KELLAN: FIREBRAND COWBOYS

BARB HAN

TORJAKE PUBLISHING

Copyright © 2023 by Barb Han

All rights reserved.

No part of this book may be reproduced in any form or by any electronic or mechanical means, including information storage and retrieval systems, without written permission from the author, except for the use of brief quotations in a book review. Furthermore, no generative AI was used in the making of this book nor can be trained on the copyrighted work.

Editing: Ali Williams

Cover Design: Jacob's Cover Designs

Proofreading: Judicious Revisions

To Brandon, Jacob, and Tori for being the great loves of my life. I don't know how I got so lucky to have each of you in my life but I know how truly blessed I am. To Babe for being my hero, my best friend, and my place to call home. I love you with all that I am.

PROLOGUE

Kellan Firebrand tapped this thumb on the steering wheel of his pickup, sitting in the gravel driveway of his cabin. His attempts to reach his brother Travis by cell had been fruitless so far. Rumor had it that his brother was wounded in a knife fight. Kellan needed to see with his own two eyes that his brother was fine. After everything that had gone down since their grandfather's death, Kellan left nothing to chance. Besides, he'd been needing to talk to someone about his own restlessness and Travis was levelheaded. He would give sound advice.

A visit to his brother's house could kill two birds with one stone. Or, at least, that was the logic. Should he call first? Or show up unannounced?

The truck windows were down. The sun setting. The sky was the real prize of living in Texas, nothing but powder blue for miles and miles tonight. Kellan loved the sky, the land and that was about all. He'd lived in Lone Star Pass his entire life, didn't know any different.

Divorced, family in turmoil, and a year and a half shy of his fortieth birthday, Kellan played around with the idea of pulling up roots and getting the hell out of Dodge. Not just Lone Star Pass. For the first time in his life, he wondered what it would be like to start fresh in a brand-new state. Colorado? Montana? Or he could throw a dart at a map. See what came up? Preferably somewhere folks weren't familiar with the name Firebrand.

The thumb tapping intensified.

Windows down, a breeze swept through the truck.

At this point, he couldn't see that he had anything to lose if he jumped ship. What exactly did he have to keep him here other than the ranch he loved? Rumor had it his last brother was planning to get married, making Kellan the lone holdout.

The tension between him and his cousin Adam, despite attempting to make peace for the family's sake, was worse than ever and getting old. Kellan tried to warm up to the other side of the family, but a lifetime spent standing on opposite sides of just about every issue took its toll.

Then there was the whole town of Lone Star Pass that was against Kellan's side of the family tree. People stared when he went into town to grab supplies that couldn't be ordered or delivered. His mother's actions and subsequent arrest had made matters worse. He couldn't begin to understand why she'd attempted murder to gain more of the family fortune. They weren't hurting for food or shelter. They had enough.

Carrying the last name Firebrand was a curse.

To add insult to injury, Adam's side of the family had moved into and taken over their grandfather's house almost immediately after the old man's death. According to his will, they had every right. But had any one of those so-called 'good Firebrands' sat any member of his side of the family down and asked if that was okay?

Nope. Not once.

Kellan had been playing along with making amends for his brothers' sake. The charade, swallowing his words, holding back was like a volcano waiting to erupt inside his chest. He was about to blow. Would it make everything worse?

Yes.

Should he drive over to his brother's or call? Travis might not be home.

Then again, his brother's cabin was on the property. It wouldn't take more than half an hour to make the drive. He picked up his cell, pulled up Travis's name, and tapped the screen to make the call.

It rolled into voicemail.

"Hey, I was hoping to catch you. We need to talk. *I* need to talk, but—"

The call dropped, cutting the connection. Kellan bit back a curse. Of course, it did. Would his brother get the message or would the phone mess that up too? It happened. He'd make a call, expect a callback, only to find out the person on the receiving end never got the message. They weren't lying about it, either. These fancy phones weren't as reliable as they should be for how much they cost.

A crash in his equipment room shocked him out of his reverie. It was probably that damn raccoon again. The one that had been wreaking havoc and being a general pain in the backside for weeks now. He set the phone down in the cupholder to investigate. The last time it visited, the darn thing chewed an electrical cord, which could have started a fire, and chewed through a wall before leaving behind 'presents' inside the wall that stunk to high heaven.

Kellan didn't need the hassle, but Murphy's Law said more bad luck was on the way.

He banged on the door as he fished a set of keys out of his jeans pocket. "Get out of my shed." Although, *shed*, wasn't nearly fancy enough of a word for his equipment room. Considering his cabin was a one-bedroom, he didn't have a whole of storage. One side of this space kept anything that didn't fit inside his house, and the other half kept equipment and tools.

Kellan unlocked the door and then listened. Inside the shed was quiet. That was odd. Normally, the raccoon scurried around when he shouted. He'd hear its nails against the tile. Was this flooring fancy for an equipment shed? Yes. But it was built well to keep pests out. Usually.

Raccoons were demons with fur.

He jangled the keys. Startling a wild animal that might perceive itself as being cornered was responsible for the six-inch scar that ran across his chest. He'd learned the lesson as a teen when common sense had taken a vacation and he'd cornered a coyote. Needless to say, the coyote won.

Kellan slowly opened the door, banging it with the set of keys. If the raccoon saw his or her exit, it would most likely escape.

There was nothing, not a sound.

Kellan stepped inside as he flicked on the overhead light. Damn raccoon must have chewed the chord because nothing happened. He muttered a string of choice words under his breath. Shelves on the righthand side of the room held several varieties of flashlights and battery-operated camping lamps.

He'd made a trail through the middle of the room the last time he was in here looking for wire cutters, shoving chairs and stacking cabinets to the side. Murphy's Law kicked in again because that was the side of the room he needed to get to in order to have light.

It dawned on him that the cell phone in his pocket had a flashlight app feature. And then he immediately realized he'd left the phone inside his truck.

There was very little daylight to draw on at this point, so the opened door did him no good. There was also a window to his right but he'd pushed a dresser up against that side.

Taking a step, he immediately drew his foot back. The shot he'd taken to the shin hurt like hell. What was in the way?

He bent down to feel around as the door to the shed closed behind him. He heard the latch close, essentially locking him in.

The lock wouldn't be able to do that on its own. Someone had to be out there.

"Hey!" Kellan turned and hopped over to the door on his good leg, slamming his fist into it. He drew his hand back immediately and released a string of curses. If this was some kind of joke, it wasn't funny. "What the hell is going on?" He was in no mood for practical jokes. Though, he didn't know anyone who would pull a stunt like this and think it was funny.

Silence on the outside of the shed sent an eerie feeling over him, like dark gray clouds engulfing a treetop moments before a severe storm.

And then he smelled it...smoke. With his cell inside the cab of his vehicle, he had no way to call for help. With smoke filling the room, he had no time.

The window.

He pulled his shirt over his nose and mouth before feeling his way over to the dresser. Smoke was already seeping through the cotton of his shirt, causing his nose and throat to burn. And then he heard a noise toward the back of the room.

The raccoon?

Was he seriously still holding onto the fantasy a raccoon was responsible for locking him into his own equipment shed?

Dismissing the noise as probably a scurrying mouse, he chucked furniture pieces out of the way as he cleared the path to the window. The dresser was heavy as hell. It had taken him and his brother to move it to the spot where it sat now, blocking his exit. It was tall, though. Could he topple it over? Kellan had to dig deep but he managed to scoot it out of the way.

And then a familiar, if faint, female voice cut through the smoke.

"Help me."

1

Of all the ways Kellan Firebrand could have expected to die, being burned alive in his equipment shed had never even made the list.

"Please help," a familiar voice begged once again from the back corner of the room. A woman. He couldn't come up with a name, though.

Another crash sounded.

Thick, black smoke burned his eyes and nose, despite the layer of cotton shirt he'd pulled over most of his face. Kellan blinked away the tears leaking from his ducts, blurring his vision.

In one minute, he'd been out in his truck waiting for word his brother Travis had survived a knife fight. In the next, he was locked inside a burning equipment room that belonged to him.

"Hold on," he said through a coughing jag.

It was dark as pitch inside and held more furniture than equipment, leftovers from his divorce that he couldn't keep in the house and couldn't get rid of.

He cursed the fact he'd left his cell inside his truck. He

pivoted toward the direction of the voice and immediately tripped over something—a boxed fan?—catching himself before he bit it with a hand on the corner of a nightstand. He steadied himself on his feet and then pulled his left hand back, shaking it. His wrist hurt like the dickens.

He cleared the fan and whatever else was on the floor by kicking it to one side before finding concrete flooring again, then took an exaggerated step up and over for good measure.

"Who's here?" he asked, figuring the unknown woman might not answer, but at this point he'd rather go for broke in case he got lucky.

"It's me, Kellan," the woman said, like he should know who the raspy voice belonged to.

Hold on a minute. Did he?

And then it dawned on him a second before he reached the back wall. "Kelsey Sheppard?" Correction, Kelsey Hightower. But then, he'd lost track of her a long time ago after she married a jerk from high school, so Kellan had no idea what name she went by these days.

They could get reacquainted once they got the hell out of there alive.

"Take my hand," he managed to say through a burning throat to the figure in the dark who now had a name. Kelsey, a.k.a. Missed Opportunity.

"I can barely see my own, let alone yours," she stated through a cough. He assumed she didn't have a cell phone, or she would have said something or called 911 by now.

A curtain of thick smoke fell in between them. Kellan reached, found her hand, ignored the surprising zing of electricity that shot through his fingertips, and linked their fingers. After pulling her to standing, she hopped on one foot.

There was no time to ask about her injury, why she was back in town, or what she'd been up to since marrying the High School Jerk and then immediately moving away. But despite that, he couldn't help the questions crowding his brain: Was said jerk responsible for her current situation? Alone and hiding? Was he responsible for the limp? All kinds of thoughts bounced through his head that made his left hand curl into a fist.

The questions mounting in his mind had to be shelved for now as the thick smoke made it hard to breathe without more coughing. Smoke inhalation killed more folks than the actual fire.

"There's a window," he managed to say as he let go of her hand and wrapped an arm around her waist to practically carry her. They were running out of time.

As sleep tugged at the back of his mind, Kellan kicked his way over to the window. Giving in to the fog in his brain meant never waking up again. Fire to a rancher was right up there with one of the worst possible things that could happen. Barns and dry hay made for quick tinder.

As the brain fog threatened to push out all rational thought, he zeroed in on one thing; the fire extinguisher he'd placed inside the shed. He was almost certain he'd left it in here. Ranchers kept them everywhere within easy reach.

"Stay here, okay?" Setting Kelsey down on the nightstand, he felt his way, navigating the items blocking his path to the door. Keeping calm, thinking clearly would keep them alive.

But where was the extinguisher?

Had he moved it?

Panic fought for center stage as he blindly felt around, moving object after object. Was he wasting time? He didn't have a clear memory of moving the extinguisher but that didn't mean he hadn't.

Just as he was about to give up, his hand found the sturdy, metal cylinder. It was too early to celebrate. Kelsey could no longer be heard over the crackling noise of the fire. Was he too late?

Kellan pulled the metal safety pin and squeezed the lever on top of the cylinder, then aimed low. White foam blasted out as he moved his arms in a sweeping motion, making a beeline toward the window area.

The second lucky break of the evening came when he put the last of the blaze out near the window. Kellan shrugged out of his flannel jacket, then swung it around in the air, using it to break up the smoke.

Coughing, eyes burning, he picked up a lamp and broke the window.

"We need to get out now, Kelsey," he said. The sounds of her coughing reassured him she was still alive.

Kellan knew enough about fires to realize only about half survived smoke inhalation. Meaning neither one of them were out of the woods yet. He could only pray there hadn't been too much exposure on either of their parts as he moved next to Kelsey again. Getting her out the window to safety was his top priority.

A thought struck. Kelsey had been hiding from someone who'd tried to kill them. Where was the bastard? Outside?

"My ankle," she said, as she put some of her weight on him to hop toward the window.

He helped her climb up and out, not thrilled at the possibility the perp who'd tried to barbecue them might be waiting on the other side.

Kelsey suppressed most of her scream as she landed on

the ground with a thud. At least she was outside in the fresh air. Her constant cough was concerning, though.

Kellan climbed out of the window next, taking the fire extinguisher with him in case he needed to use it like a baseball bat against an attacker. He launched himself away from Kelsey, who was still on the ground on her side curled in the fetal position. She held onto her ankle, wincing in pain.

Before he could give full attention to her, he scanned the area to see if the person who'd locked them inside and set the fire had stuck around to see if the job was done.

Kellan didn't see anyone but that didn't mean no one watched them from the tree line. This area of the Firebrand cattle ranch had been picked for his personal home because of its remote location. Being as far away from the family as possible suited him just fine. The less interaction he had, the better. The isolation also made for an easier target, he realized. No one would hear a scream.

All the Firebrand grandsons lived on the ranch. He was no exception despite the rising tensions between him and his cousins. There was security, ranch hands, and a foreman. Any of whom could be near the area. Or was that wishful thinking?

Out of the smoke, his brain fog cleared. Was his truck still running? Was it still parked in the driveway? If so, could he grab his cell and call for help?

Kelsey was struggling, so he went to her first. She looked up at him with the most beautiful pair of violet eyes. Silky raven hair splayed out across the thorny grass. Curiosity had him glancing at her ring finger. Another jolt of electricity fired through him when he saw no band and no tan line.

Not every married person wore a wedding ring. Case in point, his father never had. It occurred to him that might be a guy thing. Either way, there was no time to dig deeper into her personal life.

Sirens sounded in the distance. Had someone noticed the smoke and called the fire department? Emergency services? The law?

Head of security Steven Paine might have been patrolling the area or ranch foreman Bronc Harris. One of his cousins, maybe. Either way, he was thankful help was on the way.

"Who did this to you?" he asked, skimming Kelsey for injuries beyond what she might have sustained during the jump. She was beautiful by anyone's standards. Large eyes rimmed with thick, black lashes. Those same eyes were filled with fear as she sat up, holding onto her right ankle as her face twisted in pain.

"We can't stay here," she said. "We have to go or he'll come back for me."

"Who, Kelsey?" Kellan searched her face. "Your husband?"

She shook her head.

Was she divorced? A widow? If he found her sitting on his lawn right now in her current condition, Kellan would have been concerned she'd hit her head and become disoriented. Wild eyes searched the area and she curled up in a defensive posture.

"I don't know who he is," she admitted, reaching new panic levels based on her expression. "And I can't stay in one place for long or he'll find me again."

"Is there a reason anyone would be chasing you?"

"Stalking," she corrected. "He's been stalking me for weeks. I didn't know where to go, so I thought I could lose him if I disappeared here for a few days."

"He followed you to Lone Star Pass?" he asked. Her

father, the town's pastor, had passed away. Was she home for the funeral?

"Ran me off the road a couple miles back," she said, hugging her knees into her chest. There was something instinctual about curling into a ball to protect vital organs when you were under threat.

"Why didn't you immediately go to the law?" Kellan asked, figuring that was his next move. Get to his cell inside his truck and make the call to the sheriff.

"I did back in Dallas," she said on a sharp sigh. "Turns out, there's not a lot they can do when you have no idea who is stalking you, no proof of said stalking, and no way to identify the person other than to say, a medium height, stocky built dude who wears a ski mask keeps following you."

Kellan's hands fisted as a fire truck roared up to the scene. "You said he ran you off the road?"

"Guess being in a remote area worked against me," she said before sniffing away a tear.

"The bastard rammed your car and tried to kill you," Kellan said. "The situation has changed."

He had more questions than answers, along with an inconvenient attraction that had been dormant since junior year of high school.

Muscle memory. Nothing more.

Was it?

"Stay here while I grab my phone and make sure the sheriff is on his way too," he said to Kelsey. It dawned on him that they would need more than firefighters and EMTs out here as soon as possible.

After a nod from her, he hopped to his feet and bolted toward his truck, the engine still humming.

The cell was gone.

~

Kelsey Sheppard nursed her ankle—broken? sprained?—as she contemplated how much information she could give Kellan about her past and why she was on the run.

The girl who'd been one of the most popular in high school because she dated the most popular guy had fallen from grace. Hardcore. The honest and upright Firebrand would turn his back on her if she told him the truth. Right? She needed help. There was nowhere else to go now that her 'stalker' had found her once again. And would continue to hunt her down until he found what he was looking for or she was dead. No witnesses. Coming back to Lone Star Pass to lurk in the shadows at her own father's funeral had been a risk. She'd known it would be. Still, she believed she could outsmart her stalker.

How much longer could she hide?

Should she turn herself in and be done with it? Then what?

The scandal would break her mother's heart. Or worse, kill her. The woman had just lost her husband.

Not to mention the men after Kelsey were mobbed up. They wouldn't allow her to live after what she'd done. Would they go after her mother first?

A knife stabbed her chest at the thought despite her history with her parents.

Kelsey's Bible Belt parents wrote her off the minute she took off with a 'heathen' would-be rockstar after graduation. She'd been the preacher's daughter, expected to walk a straight line her entire life. Her parent's plan included her marrying a missionary before spitting out three or four kids.

No, thank you.

With no money and no skills, the big city had eaten her

alive. She'd lived in roach motels and survived on Ramen noodles while her husband was out six nights a week trying to kick off his career. The love between her and Jackson, if it could be called that, had died fairly quickly. But she'd been determined to prove her parents wrong about the marriage. *Stubborn* should have been her middle name instead of Grace.

Kelsey got jobs as a barista while Jackson worked small-town bars and was on the road more than half the year. The other half of the year, he spent in a bandmate's garage making new music, which was code for drinking until he passed out.

They moved around a lot. She never kept a job longer than a year.

After living paycheck to paycheck for almost twenty years, Jackson left her for his new bass player. Said Sydney understood him in ways that Kelsey never would, after he'd been dropped from his label—his final chance at breaking in, according to his manager—following three consecutive flops. Said Sydney would never ask him to consider leaving the band to get a 'real' job just to buy a bigger house. Said Sydney understood a real musician after his once-promising career never got off the ground. He had the audacity to accuse Kelsey of staying with him for the payoff once he made it big.

She still couldn't believe the accusation. The insult was laughable. There'd been precious little money for nearly twenty years. Twenty years!

She could have survived on love and just enough money to make ends meet and been happy as a lark. Instead, pride kept her in a loveless marriage.

Jackson walking out on her had broken her at first, and then made her mad.

That was a year and a half ago. Without her knowledge before the split, he'd opened several credit cards and then maxed them out. He'd been lying about paying rent by getting the landlord to promise not to say anything to her. Jackson had the gall to say she was pregnant and he didn't want to cause undo worry. In reality, he'd been pocketing *her* hard-earned money while lying to both her and their landlord while maxing out credit cards buying Sydney anything she wanted.

The last Kelsey heard, Sydney got sick of Jackson's lying and kicked him out.

Kelsey's credit was ruined in the process, making it impossible for her to rent a decent apartment. So, for the past eighteen months, she'd picked up a second job and lived in a pay-by-the-week motel.

The racket she heard through paper-thin walls, while trying to grab a few hours of sleep in the afternoons before her night job, made her believe the place could be rented by the hour too. Needless to say, the clientele wasn't exactly the upper crust of society. Bottom feeders were more like it. In addition to passionate moans—faking it?—and choruses of, *yes, yes, yes!* there'd been awful sounds of heads being slammed into walls and meek voices begging for mercy.

Low-hum conversations of women pleading to keep a few extra bucks for basic supplies like tampons and being told he wasn't buying their excuses. If they wanted continued protection, they needed to pay for it. Otherwise, he would leave them to their own devices with their so-called clients.

Kelsey always intervened when she heard physical abuse, calling cops that were sometimes too busy and too short-staffed to show until it was all over and the women claimed they got into an argument with their boyfriend and nothing more. No charges were ever pressed.

Witnessing victim mentality firsthand should have clued her into her own situation. Kelsey had placed her marriage in a different category. She'd stayed out of stubbornness and youthful pride. And when she was no longer in her twenties, she stayed out of embarrassment. There'd been no way she was going to tuck her tail between her legs and come home to her parents. Plus, it had been easy to stay since Jackson was rarely ever around. Moving every couple of months kept her working dispensable jobs and busy enough to keep the loneliness at bay.

"Bastard took my cell," Kellan said as he jogged over, breaking through her reverie. The fact he could jog was impressive after swallowing all that smoke. Breathing made her lungs hurt.

"That's not good news," she managed to say through a throat that felt like sandpaper. Then added, "I'm sorry, Kellan."

"Not your fault," he countered.

If only he knew the truth.

"It's possible someone saw smoke," he reasoned. "But I need to get you to the hospital right now."

"I'll be fine," she said, trying to hide the panic. "I just need to wrap my ankle. It'll be okay."

Sirens wailed. They were getting close.

"Looks like help is almost here," Kellan said, scanning her again with a look of concern, causing wrinkles on his forehead. A trail of heat followed his gaze like a laser, warming her along its path. "I heard about your father, by the way." He bowed his head. "I'm sorry, Kelsey. Not that I spent much time in his pews, but I'm sure he was a good man."

Would a good man tell his daughter she was no longer welcome in his home?

"Thank you, Kellan," she said, unable to speak badly of her father now. Did his words that day after graduation hurt? They'd been the equivalent of multiple stab wounds right through the heart. But actually being disowned had broken her further.

Kelsey's stubborn streak was just as long as her father's, though, according to her mother. And she'd dug her heels in deep to stay with Jackson.

Had she inherited the trait from her father like her mother believed?

"I'm guessing that's the reason you came back after all these years," Kellan said as he continued to scan the area.

"It is," she admitted as a fire truck pulled up. Not a minute later, emergency personnel flooded the area.

If she could get up and run, she would. How was she going to explain her situation? Keep with the stalker story?

Kelsey couldn't let her secret get out. Her mother's life might depend on it as much as her own.

Could she keep running?

2

In a matter of minutes, Kellan had an oxygen mask strapped over his nose and mouth as he was being examined and questioned by EMT Joey Smith. Joey looked barely out of high school. Like he didn't even shave yet. Was he old enough to know what he was doing?

When had Kellan become so old?

Staring down his fortieth birthday with a divorce under his belt wasn't exactly where he thought he would be at this point in life. But right now, his problems seemed small compared to Kelsey's stalker—a stalker who'd tried to kill her and anyone who tried to help her.

She was already strapped to a gurney, oxygen mask secured, being wheeled toward the back of an ambulance and an uncertain future now that the bastard had disappeared. Joey needed to finish up so Kellan could follow her to the hospital to get more information. Possibly even help her.

Seeing Kelsey again was certainly a blast from the past. Suddenly, Kellan was back in high school, too nervous to ask her out junior year, even after the night at the lake when he thought she'd given him signs. A week later, he finally drummed up enough courage to ask her out before discovering Jackson Hightower beat him to the punch. After that, the two remained a couple throughout high school and beyond.

No offense to Kelsey but she'd married a jerk.

Jackson might have been popular in high school for the band he'd been in that played gigs in Austin but it was common knowledge he cheated on Kelsey often. In fact, he developed a reputation for breaking up with her on a Thursday so he could have a guilt-free hookup weekend while he played a gig only to ask her back on Monday.

For reasons Kellan would never understand, she took the guitar player back. Had Jackson been popular? Yes. Had he been the 'it' kid back in high school? Yes. Had he hit his peak in those years and the few following high school? Yes.

Kellan didn't care one way or the other. He overheard folks in town mentioning the 'Hightower boy' as he'd been referred to as falling from grace after what had been a promising start in music.

Kellan pulled his mask away from his face so he could address Joey directly while the 'kid' explained he was putting a gadget on Kellan's finger to check his pulse ox. He stifled the question he wanted to ask, *How old are you,* instead settling for, "Where is Kelsey being taken?"

"Lone Star General," Joey said, not a wrinkle in sight on his baby face. Being this close to someone so young made Kellan feel ancient. The kid looked like he worked out, though. What Joey lacked in height he made up for in bulk. EMTs needed to be strong to lift patients, so it made sense he would be strong and fit.

"I can drive myself as soon as I get the all-clear," Kellan said, not hiding his impatience at the man-child.

Something told him that Kelsey wasn't being completely honest about her situation, and he needed to know why. She was holding back. Was she afraid? Distrustful? Kellan couldn't quite put his finger on it.

Either way, a serious crime had been committed on Kellan's property, so he was now involved and intended to see this through, whatever *this* turned out to be.

Seeing those violet eyes full of fear had pulled on his protective instincts. He couldn't rightly walk away from her if he could help. Ranchers weren't built that way. At least, that was the lie he told himself, instead of owning up to the fact he'd had a serious crush on Kelsey back in high school, and he was now curious how her life had turned out.

And she no longer wore a wedding ring and had picked up a stalker, which confused Kellan because the gossip mill said she was happily married, touring Europe with Jackson. It didn't add up. At this point, Kellan figured she needed a friend. Besides, the moment they'd shared junior year before she became Jackson Hightower's girlfriend had caused questions to linger.

Questions that made him wonder how life would have turned out if he'd plucked up the courage to ask her out in the week between thinking they'd shared a moment and Jackson asking her out.

"With your pulse ox level, you could pass out behind the wheel," Joey insisted. "Let one of us drive and we'll make certain you get to the hospital in one piece. I guarantee it. Go on your own and it could end badly. Meaning, you'd end up in my ambulance anyway and possibly in much worse shape."

Considering the fact he'd taken in lungs full of deadly smoke, he decided not to disagree with the wet-behind-the-ears EMT. Besides, despite being young, he clearly knew what he was talking about.

Before Kellan could answer one way or the other his cousin Adam came roaring up in his pickup, causing a dust storm. The cloud broke as Adam came bolting over with a serious look on his face.

"I got a call from security that there was a fire," Adam said as he stopped next to Joey.

"I'll live," Kellan reassured, figuring it might have been Paine who'd seen the smoke. Kellan and Adam hadn't exactly been on the best of terms recently, or ever. Kellan had been doing his best to keep peace with his cousins but was still bothered by the fact Adam had taken over their grandfather's home after his death. Adam had every right, according to the will, but he hadn't given the other side of the family the courtesy of asking if they minded. Both sides should have had rights to the Marshal's home if anyone asked Kellan. Since they hadn't and technically didn't have to, Kellan didn't have a legitimate reason to complain. It still rubbed him the wrong way.

He looked his cousin directly in the eyes, thanked him for showing up, and told Joey to load him up in the damn ambulance.

"I can follow," Adam offered as his cell tones rang out. He mumbled an apology as he checked the screen. "It's my wife. I should take this."

"Better yet, go home to her," Kellan insisted. "I'll be in and out of the hospital in no time."

Adam clamped his lips shut like he was stopping himself from saying something. He answered the phone and immediately asked his wife to hold. He turned his attention back to Kellan, then paused. He looked like he was debating his next move carefully. "Fine. I won't go to the hospital. Can we at least stock the fridge?"

"I never turn down a meal," Kellan said before Joey not-so-gently asked him to put the mask back on. Kellan made a show of letting go of the mask. A mistake, considering it snapped against his face. Hard. What could he say? He was his own worst enemy when it came to his temper—a temper that he'd been working on getting under control because yelling at everyone, it turned out, got everyone riled up and very little accomplished.

Adam half-smiled before turning his attention back to the phone and his wife. He took a couple of steps in the opposite direction.

"Is she okay?" he asked low into the receiver, sounding concerned.

Was something wrong with Angel?

The little girl was Adam's biological daughter. Prudence, his wife, had stepped in to become the mother the little girl needed. Angel's biological mother died, leaving Adam unaware he'd fathered a child who was a few months old at the time. The term *it's complicated* applied to most of the Firebrands. Adam and Prudence were blissfully happy with their little family.

And he'd been making an effort with Kellan's side of the family in recent months, which was appreciated by most. He had his own family to take care of too. What he'd done with the Marshal's house still wasn't right, but right now Kellan needed to get to the hospital so he could find out the real reason Kelsey had picked up a stalker and if she had any ideas as to the man's identity.

"Let's go," he said to Joey after pulling his mask away from his mouth so he could talk.

Favors must have been called in for Kelsey to be sharing a room with Kellan. The Firebrand name was powerful in Lone Star Pass. In all of Texas. No doubt, Kellan used his considerable pull to make the room-sharing happen. Kelsey hadn't meant to involve him in this mess she'd created. Her life had been one big miscalculation after another. Throw in the stubborn streak she'd inherited by her father and she was a disaster waiting to happen.

Used to be, she corrected. *No more.*

The EMTs who'd brought her in immediately turned her over to the floor nurse. At least she'd bypassed the ER and gone straight to a nice room. Another Firebrand favor? Had to be. Or maybe it was just special treatment that only a Firebrand would be used to in the small town of Lone Star Pass.

Her family name had put her on the receiving end of plenty of baked goods during the holidays, but that was where the special treatment ended. With all the high expectations of holiness that came with being a preacher's daughter, Kelsey had learned to grin and bear all the scrutiny. By her eighteenth birthday, she'd been all smiled out. The town had become claustrophobic. And she'd been bent on proving her parents wrong about her marriage to Jackson.

Kelsey sighed. She had news for Lone Star Pass, she was far from innocent. Keeping the information about her activities from making its way back to her mother along the grapevine that came with small towns was the least she could do after defying her parents and making a mess of her life. Everyone thought they knew her, the smiling, well-behaved preacher's kid who 'sang like an angel' at Christmas and Easter services. As much as she'd loved to sing, getting up in front of people was the scariest thing in the world to her. Won't they all be shocked now when they find out how her life had turned out?

Before she could open the curtain between her and Kellan to ask him to let her do the talking, Sheriff Timothy Lawler followed the doctor onto her side of the room. The sheriff had been two grades ahead in school, so she knew of him. She'd passed him in the halls and attended a few football games where he'd been the starting quarterback.

Kelsey remembered her father visiting the Lawler's home after Timothy, who'd been a star being scouted by some big-name programs, endured a career-ending hit that broke his arm in four places. The senior Mr. Lawler, who'd been sheriff at the time, often bragged that his son had managed to get off the game winning throw. But the injury had cost him a football career.

Apparently, he'd recovered and gone to college to study criminal justice before following in his father's footsteps in law enforcement.

The younger Lawler was about as fair-skinned as they came. He had ginger hair that was in a military cut. He had a hawk-like nose and compassionate brown eyes. He wore jeans, boots, and a tan shirt with the word, Sheriff, embroidered on the right front pocket.

His presence scared the hell out of her.

There was no way she could tell him what really happened or what was really going on. Would Kellan give her away?

"The sheriff wants to ask a few questions while the information is fresh in your mind," the doctor said after introducing himself as Dr. Guerra. "We negotiated to allow him to do his job, as long as it doesn't interfere with me doing mine."

She pointed to her oxygen mask and shrugged. Then, to her throat, which still burned like it had been set on fire instead of the shed.

"You can lift the mask only when necessary to answer," Dr. Guerra said.

At least she had an ally with the good doctor. Kelsey could work it to her advantage.

"Point to where you're feeling the most pain," Dr. Guerra said after studying her chart for a moment. His gaze swept the data, stopping only occasionally. He pressed his lips together at the stops, which she took as his 'tell' that he didn't like what he saw.

Kelsey motioned toward her right ankle.

"I'm going to send you down for x-rays on that ankle," Dr. Guerra said as he hooked the chart on the end of the bed. "Let me take a look." He removed the cover. Her shoe was already off. At some point, maybe in the ambulance, her shoe had been removed and bagged.

Sitting up, she could see the bruising already happening, as well as the swelling.

Dr. Guerra turned his head slightly to a nurse who'd appeared next to him seemingly out of nowhere like a poltergeist. "Let's get a cold compress on this. See if we can help ease some of the discomfort." He paused for a few seconds. "Elevate as well."

"Yes, sir," the nurse stated, picking up the file and taking note. Her nametag was being blocked, so Kelsey had no idea who the nurse could be. But the woman scurried around and had a cold compress on the ankle in what felt like a matter of seconds, her movements fluid like this exact moment had been rehearsed dozens of times.

Kelsey realized she'd become suspicious of just about everyone over the last few months. Then again, hitting rock bottom and compromising what was left of your morals by getting involved in illegal activity had a way of stripping your trust in others. The truth about the reason she didn't trust law enforcement couldn't get out.

Where did you go when the law was after you?

"It's been a long time, Mrs. Hightower," Sheriff Lawler began, taking a step around Dr. Guerra. "I'm sorry about your father. He was a good man."

Of course, the sheriff would remember the preacher's daughter. Kelsey half smiled and gave a nod of acknowledgment. She mouthed a *thank you*. Then, she lifted her mask. "It's back to Sheppard now." Talking hurt. Her throat felt like it closed up after someone rubbed sandpaper on it.

Taking back her name had been the only bright spot in the divorce. Getting her life back was supposed to be the other. Now? After what she'd done?

Kelsey stopped herself from going down that road again. *What's done is done.*

No amount of regret could magically send her back in time so she could handle the situation differently. Desperate times had called for desperate measures. She'd had to do what she could in order to keep a roof over her head and put food on the table while barely scraping by. She'd been one misstep away from homelessness.

Lawler had a notepad underneath his arm. He set it down on the tray table along with a pen he'd fished out of his shirt pocket. "I understand speaking is difficult. Would you mind writing down the answers to my questions instead?"

So much for getting out of giving a statement.

Kelsey should have known the sheriff would have something like this up his sleeve. Getting out of giving a full statement didn't look to be in the cards.

Panic struck at the thought of being taken down for an x-ray, leaving the sheriff and Kellan alone. She'd mentioned a stalker to Kellan because nothing better had come to mind. She assumed it would shut down any questions he might have before he asked them. Now, she would have to commit to the story.

Kelsey hated lying. She hated liars. Could she come clean? Tell the sheriff everything and ask for a deal to protect her mother?

No, because her mother would be found and tortured and Kelsey would be as good as dead. The men she'd gotten mixed up with had connections to even bigger criminals and the law.

Unbeknownst to her at the time, she'd brought this on herself.

3

Kellan listened closely to what was happening on the other side of the curtain. If Kelsey wrote down her answers, he would remain in the dark. Would she be treated and released before he got to the bottom of why she'd been on his property inside his shed? She'd said there was a stalker but the explanation rang hollow. Wouldn't she want to go to the law if only to continue to document her case instead of coming across as afraid?

The fearful Kelsey would bolt the minute she could. That much, he could feel in his bones.

Two guys wearing white scrubs entered the room on opposite sides of a stretcher. He'd overheard the doctor speaking to a nurse. She worked fast. Then again, everything was on tablets these days. All anyone had to do was tap a screen to place an order for almost anything. Medicine would be no different.

What would the future bring? Think something and it would magically show up? The thought wasn't reassuring. The last thing the world needed was a machine anticipating needs. Big Brother eavesdropping on conversations through phones and devices was getting out of hand already.

"Is your ex-husband mad at you, or has he threatened you?" Sheriff Lawler asked. At least Kellan could hear one side of the conversation, maybe pick up clues as to what Kelsey's answers were.

She must have answered no.

"What about fights with anyone?" Sheriff Lawler continued.

Again, she must have answered no.

Was it strange that she didn't seem to be volunteering information? Then again, she'd been clear about her mistrust of law enforcement.

Kellan reasoned she'd been through a traumatic experience to say the least. The Kelsey he remembered had been quiet, shy. Except the few times she'd been put on stage to sing. The Marshal, a.k.a. Kellan's grandfather, had insisted on going to church on Christmas and Easter like they were some type of upstanding family. The man made large, conspicuous donations, so his sins washed away in a sea of green. The bonus of going for Kellan was getting to hear Kelsey sing.

"Have you recently broken up with anyone?" The questions continued from Lawler. "What about rejections? Has anyone shown interest in you that you ended up saying no to?"

More answers in the *no* column based on the line of questioning.

"Here's my information," Lawler continued after collecting basic facts about her home address and how to reach her, all of which she must have written down on the pad of paper.

The sound of a few sheets of paper being torn off and then folded signaled the end of the conversation.

"Feel free to contact me if anything else comes to mind," Lawler said.

"We really need to take her for an x-ray now, sir," one of the orderlies said.

Lawler thanked Kelsey before stepping inside the curtained area on Kellan's side of the room.

"Doesn't sound like she has a clue as to who the stalker might be," Kellan said to the sheriff.

Lawler shook his head in response. "What about you? What did you see?"

Kellan gave a quick rundown of the situation, which amounted to no idea who was behind this. "The bastard got my cell phone."

The sheriff's eyes lit up. "I have a shot at tracking that for you if you give me the number."

He rattled off the digits. "Think you can locate it? Is it really that easy?"

"Depends on a whole mess of factors," Lawler stated. "We have better luck with newer phones, but if the perp is on Firebrand land where there's no reception, we might never be able to get a good trace on it. At least, not in time to catch him. He could end up ditching the phone and disappearing by the time someone is able to set up a stingray device."

"I've had the phone for several years, so I wouldn't exactly call it new," Kellan admitted, wishing he'd bought one recently so it could be traced easier, if it meant catching the bastard who'd tried to kill him.

"I'll get someone on it," he said, tapping information into his cell, most likely in the form of a text. A few seconds later, he looked at Kellan. "What else can you tell me?"

"That's it," he admitted. "Kelsey said she was back in town for her father's funeral and that the guy following her ran her off the road."

"I didn't see her at the funeral," Sheriff Lawler said. "A few of the ladies turned up their noses saying she was 'too good' to come back for 'her own daddy's funeral'."

Kellan issued a sharp sigh. He, of all people, knew how gossipy folks could be. "I couldn't tell you one way or the other. All I know is that was the reason Kelsey gave for coming back to town. She might have thrown on a wig and sunglasses to avoid being the center of attention."

The sheriff nodded as he took note. "According to the gossip mill, Kelsey hasn't been home since she got married."

"I haven't seen her but that doesn't mean she hasn't been here," Kellan stated. He didn't get off ranch property much since he worked seven days a week. "Someone should tell them to mind their own business and stop interfering in other people's lives." Hearing that the gossip hounds were after Kelsey brought out his protective instincts. He knew how much their words stung.

"Point taken," Sheriff Lawler conceded.

His mother's situation had renewed the gossips' interest in his family. After the Marshal died, she'd concocted a murder scheme to get more of the inheritance. She'd been caught, arrested, and was awaiting trial. Now that a big-time criminal defense team had taken over the case, the trial was set to start next week. In fact, Kellan should probably be heading to Houston to support his mother. Her tragic past and issues with alcohol had distorted her sense of right and wrong. Now that she was sober and seeing clearly, she was ashamed of her actions. Jackie Firebrand also wanted to atone for what she'd done now that she was thinking straight and understood the gravity of what she'd done.

She deserved a fair trial even if she didn't think so.

Kellan intended to show support. He had a few days before he absolutely had to leave.

"Why did Kelsey's stalker try to kill me?" Kellan asked.

"It's possible you led him straight to her and would have been collateral damage," Sheriff Lawler said. "But that's a guess on my part. We won't know for certain until he's under arrest and we can fit the pieces together."

It might be conjecture but the sheriff's educated guess rang true.

"You mentioned in your statement that you went inside the shed to investigate what you thought was a raccoon," Sheriff Lawler supplied.

Something wasn't adding up. What was it?

"The stalker must believe Kelsey saw him or could give a description of him to the law or that you would save her," the sheriff continued.

She couldn't. At least not according to what she'd told Kellan.

"Or a name," Lawler continued. "She might have it in there in her brain somewhere and just can't access the information because of the trauma she experienced."

"Is that normal?" Kellan asked.

"It's not abnormal," the sheriff answered. "That's why I always give a victim my contact information. Stress and/or trauma can cause the brain to block out critical details. Later, once the victim calms down, it's not unheard of for me to get a call. Something will trigger the memory and the name pops into their mind or an important detail that pieces everything together."

Made sense to Kellan. Except for the fact Kelsey had been lucid. She'd seemed sharp as a tack. Or was that part of the deal with trauma-related forgetfulness? He had no background in brain science or reason to understand any of it beyond a basic level of human interest.

The sheriff's phone buzzed. He checked the screen. "Looks like we got a hit."

"Sounds like good news," Kellan said.

"It might be," he said after studying the screen for a few more seconds. "The cell's location has been pinpointed to an area on the ranch about a hundred yards from your home."

Kellan removed the oxygen mask, threw off covers, and dropped his feet onto the cold tile.

"Hold on a minute," Sheriff Lawler warned, putting a hand up to stop Kellan from making a beeline for the door. "The first priority is to make certain you're out of the woods health-wise."

"I feel fine," Kellan argued.

"You do for now," Sheriff Lawler pointed out. "Leave here and something happens..."

Kellan had no plans to give an inch on this one. "I'm aware of the risks, Sheriff."

"The perp might be long gone, Kellan. You'd be risking your own health for nothing if that was the case."

The sheriff's honesty caused Kellan to sit back down. His temper tried to take the wheel, but he reminded himself how poorly that worked out. Instead of running off half-cocked, he issued another sharp sigh and put the damn mask back on.

Being here allowed him to keep an eye on Kelsey.

"I promise to do my job," Lawler continued. "I have a deputy close to your home who is going to check it out right now. The second he finds your phone or the perp, or both, he'll contact me."

In the end, the main reason Kellan decided to stay put

was Kelsey. If she remembered a name, he wanted to be here to hear it. The bastard responsible crossed a line when he brought this fight to Kellan's doorstep. Kelsey was the key. Keeping her close was his priority.

"With your permission, the deputy can inspect inside your home too," the sheriff said as an orderly came rushing into the room. The sheriff opened the curtain all the way, giving Kellan a view to the whole room.

"What's wrong?" Sheriff Lawler asked.

"Nothing," the orderly said, shaking his head. "It's just weird. That's all."

"What's weird?"

Sheriff Lawler must have shot the orderly a look as he doubled back toward the door because the man stopped in his tracks.

"We lost our patient," the orderly said. "Thought she might have come back to her room."

"By herself?" Sheriff Lawler asked.

The orderly's face pinched as he realized how that must sound after he'd been one of two people who'd wheeled her out of here.

Kellan didn't bother asking questions. He recalled the look of fear on Kelsey's face. There was no way she was staying in this hospital like a sitting duck. She'd gotten the hell out of there and wasn't coming back.

～

KELSEY HAD nothing but her legs to carry her. But if she could somehow get back to her vehicle before the law found it or the dude trying to catch her or kill her, she might just be able to get out of Lone Star Pass in one piece.

Being left alone in the hallway while an orderly took a

bathroom break—something she was certain he would get in trouble for later—she'd taken the opportunity to climb off the gurney and hop down the hallway. She stopped off at a supply room closet and grabbed tape to wrap her ankle, stuffed a roll inside her pocket. There was no time to search for a compression sock, which would be ideal. The unlocked room—another lucky break—didn't have anything she could take for pain. No surprise there. Painkillers would be locked up. The cold press the nurse had put on before Kelsey was wheeled out of the room numbed the injury. It didn't do much for the swelling since she'd barely had it on, but that was to be expected.

She glanced around, wishing there was a set of scrubs tucked away somewhere. No luck there. She'd noticed the cameras too. Chin to chest, she avoided looking directly at them.

Getting out of the hospital without drawing attention might be tricky. Her best move would be to fake confidence. The move went a long way toward convincing others. Turned out, confidence didn't have to be real to be convincing. Still, she wished there was a way to keep her face hidden from the cameras.

Time was of the essence, so she went for it, knowing full well a camera was going to get her at some point. She couldn't worry about it. Besides, everyone would know she ditched the hospital soon enough.

So, chin up, chest out, it was.

This time, it worked magic as she walked out of storage, to the elevator, and then out the double glass doors of the ER. The attendant never once looked up from the computer screen.

The crisp night air bit through her light sweater and jeans. Her shoes had been removed; the cement cold on her stockinged feet. Going back to the room wasn't even a remote possibility with Kellan inside.

It had been a mistake to come to Lone Star Pass. She realized that now, a little too late.

After being crashed into and run off the road in her car, she'd abandoned everything, including her handbag, to run away. There'd been no time to grab her cell, which was inside her vehicle too. At least, it had been. She had no idea if it was still there.

Times like this made her realize just how lost she was without her phone, how dependent she'd become on a device that was not bigger than her flat hand, yet held her life together. Everything she needed was in that phone: numbers, apps that could summon a ride, her credit card information.

Couldn't be helped. She needed another plan now.

Leaving Kellan without an explanation made her feel like a jerk, but telling him the truth wasn't an option either. No one could know what she'd done, and not just to save herself from embarrassment.

Kellan would end up a target. It was best to let *them* believe she didn't know Kellan at all. That driving down that road hadn't been a bout of nostalgia but simply a ride through the town where she grew up after her father died. Taking the long way around town helped her avoid all the gawks and questions from busybodies who needed to mind their own business.

In truth, seeing Kellan again caused the last twenty years to dissipate like early morning fog after the sun broke through. The night they'd spent together at the lake after the football game, before Jackson swooped in and asked her out, had been the sweetest of her life. She'd thought Kellan was interested in dating, seeing where their connection went. But he'd never even spoken to her again after that night.

Firebrands were the cool kids aside from her boyfriend, so she should have seen it coming. Kellan had most likely been filling time with her. Meanwhile, she'd read so much into it that she'd convinced herself he was about to ask her out. Not just to date, either. The vibe she'd picked up—or so she'd believed—had been the real thing. Something that could last.

How naïve was that? How silly was she? How embarrassed was she?

Even now she felt a current run between them that couldn't be explained as anything other than mutual attraction.

Once again, she was probably misreading the signs. There was no way Kellan Firebrand thought of her as anything but a person in need. As a rancher, the man was concerned for her safety in the same way he would be for anyone who showed up on his property in a difficult situation. It was rancher code. She'd grown up around them, she would know firsthand what their generosity was like.

Plus, the 'stalker' who'd been chasing her had tried to kill Kellan too. He wouldn't want to walk away from that, which was the reason she'd had to run.

One thing was clear to her now, though. Under no circumstances could she bring her past to Kellan's doorstep. He wouldn't give up. He would expose them both and end up getting killed.

She couldn't do that to him or his family. Yes, she'd checked for a ring and didn't find one. She'd wanted to ask if he had a wife and kid inside the home she'd come across while ditching the bastard who ran her off the road and then continued to chase her. The only advantage she'd had over the person who'd been one step behind was growing up in the area and knowing the land better.

Otherwise...

Kelsey didn't want to think about what might have happened. As it was, she had smoke damage in her lungs, which was winding her more than she cared to acknowledge as she walked into the cold evening of the parking lot. Not to mention her ankle pain, which was most likely nothing more than a high ankle sprain instead of a break, though it hadn't been confirmed with an x-ray since she'd bolted. She could work with a sprain. A break was a whole different beast.

Bracing against the wind, Kelsey hugged her arms to her chest and braved the cold as she searched for a means to get far away from the hospital.

4

"You lost your patient?" Kellan could scarcely believe the words coming out of his own mouth. "How exactly did that happen?"

"Restroom break," the orderly said, cheeks stained red with embarrassment.

Kellan removed the oxygen mask. He had a feeling if he lost track of Kelsey, she would disappear and never come back. The stalker who was after her might just succeed in killing her this time. "When did this go down?"

"It's been a few minutes, maybe ten," the orderly stated.

Kellan took one look at Sheriff Lawler, who was already texting a message, most likely to get someone on the streets to search for Kelsey.

"Then, she can't have gone far," Kellan said pulling monitors off his chest before hopping off the bed and putting on his boots. His clothes were still on. He assumed Kelsey's were as well. Although, the EMT who'd worked on her would have likely cut the leg of her jeans open.

"She might still be inside the hospital," Sheriff Lawler pointed out.

"I'll alert security," the orderly said with an apology.

As frustrated as Kellan might be, the orderly had no idea Kelsey would bolt if he took his eyes off her long enough. Hell, the move had caught both Kellan and the sheriff off guard. The orderly didn't have a chance of predicting it.

Sheriff Lawler put a hand to Kellan's chest to stop him from making a run for the door. "You sure this is a good idea?"

"Searching for Kelsey?" Kellan asked. "Never been more certain of anything."

"They have you in here for a reason," Sheriff Lawler pointed out. "I can handle searching for her."

"I'm not going to get any rest in here while she's out there, scared half out of her wits, running on a bad ankle and no shoes," Kellan said. He didn't point out the fact she'd shown up at his place. For help? Or was that a coincidence?

He hoped not.

Kellan wanted to help Kelsey. They had a history, however short. Plus, the fear in her eyes when he'd first found her would haunt him for the rest of his days if she ended up dead.

"I don't know how helpful I'll be out there," he said honestly. "But I know that I won't be any in here."

"Fair enough," Sheriff Lawler stated before dropping his hand. "I don't have to tell you that your family has been through too much already."

"We appreciate everything you've done on our behalf," Kellan said as they exited the room together.

"Good people deserve a break," the sheriff said. The man had no idea how much Kellan appreciated hearing those words when he figured the law must hate them by now. His side of the family wasn't always on the receiving end of praise like Adam's.

"Means a lot to hear you say that, Sheriff."

Lawler tipped his Stetson in a show of respect. "I'll work this floor, in case she's hiding in a closet somewhere."

"My guess is that she made it all the way out of the building," Kellan said. "She won't have anywhere to go and doesn't have any money, which could make her an easy target."

The sheriff nodded.

"She's resourceful," Kellan said after a thoughtful pause. She didn't have shoes, which might cause folks to believe she would stay inside. Of course, she would do the opposite because it was the least logical place she would go.

A person who jumped off a gurney to escape a hospital worker who was trying to help her wouldn't do something so normal as stay in the warmth of the building. No, she would bolt into the chilly night in only socks on her feet because it was the least logical move possible.

An argument could be made for sticking around the hospital, hiding in someone else's room on a different floor. Or, possibly in an unlocked supply closet. Would she have found scrubs? Some other way to disguise herself?

Following along with that logic, she could have sneaked into someone's room and taken shoes too. He wished he'd thought to grab hers from the room before he set out. Although he was already improving, the brain fog from the smoke wasn't helping when he had to rush a decision.

Kellan checked the faces of each person as he passed in the hallway and then the elevator. Security was on the lookout for Kelsey. They would likely cover the parking lot as well as the building.

But how many were on staff in a small hospital? It seemed like budgets were being cut everywhere. The hospital would be no exception. Top threats that came to mind in this environment were infant abductions, patients assaulting medical personnel, and—what else?—property theft. The infant floor would likely have extra security. Cameras?

He glanced up and located one almost immediately.

Good. The sheriff would cover that ground.

Was Kelsey savvy enough to keep her face hidden from view?

Cameras were getting clearer and clearer, so it was possible Kelsey could be identified. Sheriff Lawler would know if she left the building, which made more and more sense the longer Kellan thought about it.

Who would stick around with all these recording devices?

Was Kelsey afraid her stalker would find her at the hospital? Was that the reason she'd bolted at her first opportunity? She feared the stalker would catch up to her?

The sheriff could have placed someone at the door to protect her. She mentioned losing all trust in law enforcement back in Dallas, but this was Lone Star Pass. Despite everything that had happened and was still happening, folks still looked out for each other. Didn't they?

Kellan had seen it with his siblings and cousins. He'd also seen the flip side of the so-called good people of his town. The judgmental side. The side that was quick to accuse. The side that made up their minds about someone, making it impossible to break free from the made-up story.

Kelsey grew up here. She would know firsthand how the townsfolk could be. It dawned on him that a stalker might be one reason she'd decided to keep a low profile during her visit. The other would be the fact she'd been on the wrong end of gossip years ago. Didn't he remember hearing something about a falling out between her and her parents over getting married?

Twenty years was a long time ago. Funny how the brain chose to keep some memories, discard others. Because now that he really thought about it, the Marshal had made a few derogatory comments about the preacher's daughter after she moved out of town.

If being a Firebrand meant having expectations placed on Kellan since birth, he couldn't imagine how much more intense the magnifying glass must have been for Kelsey.

Damn. No wonder she got married young and got the hell out of town.

Kellan made it outside in a matter of minutes. The fact he was breathing normally gave him hope there was no serious damage to his lungs from smoke inhalation. There was a possibility that Kelsey wasn't in as good a shape as him. The thought of her curled up somewhere in the night, gasping for air while slowly dying hit him with the equivalent force of a punch to the solar plexus.

There were a couple dozen vehicles, both cars and trucks, in the lot by the ER. Kellan took a chance going out the way they'd come in, figuring it was the path she knew. It made sense that Kelsey would exit the same way she came in. It was faster. She didn't have a whole lot of time to debate her next move. Every second risked getting caught. Kellan gambled on familiarity. Hoped the move would pay off.

A flash of light in the distance that almost looked like a firefly from here caught his attention. Folks in Lone Star Pass had a habit of leaving their keys inside their vehicles. Recent events changed the behavior for Firebrands, and since there'd been many recent crimes in the area, he hoped others had followed suit.

There was a possibility that he was about to scare the bejesus out of a stranger, but his money was on Kelsey needing shelter and, if someone was careless enough, free transportation.

Stepping off the curb, he would find out soon enough.

Movement from the opposite side of the parking lot caught Kellan's eye. A dark, hooded figure was moving toward the same vehicle as Kellan.

He picked up the pace.

∽

Kelsey was so cold she could hear her own teeth chatter as she slipped into the backseat of the Ford Taurus. There was a sweater in the back, thank the stars. She immediately put it on and was swathed in that salty smell she recalled from hugging her grandmother when she'd been alive. It was the scent of dancing around the kitchen with broomsticks while an apple pie baked in the oven. It was the aroma of flannel nightgowns mixed with cinnamon covering an apron. And it was the fragrance of unconditional love wrapped in marshmallows and hot cocoa on a cold night.

Speaking of whom, Granny would have strung Kelsey's parents by their ankles and hung them upside-down on the front lawn if she'd been around. Sadly, Kelsey lost her favorite ally the summer before junior year.

At least she was out of the biting wind. Her ankle throbbed with pain—the kind of throbbing where she could feel every beat of her heart in that ankle.

Was she safe for the night? Could she rest? Regroup?

Once everyone realized she was no longer inside the hospital, would they assume she'd left the area? Gone back to her vehicle?

More panic set in because she needed to get there first if she was going to get her belongings back. Without a purse, credit cards, or phone she wouldn't last long out here in the cold. Forget the fact she couldn't walk two steps without freezing her toes off. Too bad there wasn't a pair of spare sneakers on the floorboard.

For now, though, she was safe. The law couldn't check every single vehicle in the parking lot. Plus, it made no sense she would climb into a stranger's vehicle. Right?

Doubting her actions meant admitting she might be even more vulnerable if she stuck around. There was no way she could cross the large field to her left without being caught. It was too flat, too easy to spot a runner.

Runner?

Kelsey used that term loosely. She couldn't jog let alone run. Her ankle looked like Shrek's at this point. Walking out of the parking lot might be pushing it, which was exactly the reason she'd picked the vehicle. That, and for shelter. The sweater had been an unexpected bonus but she remembered how common it was for folks to keep a blanket, sweater, or hoodie in the backseat. No one could ever be too sure they wouldn't need it for something. That had been Granny's philosophy.

Kelsey breathed in more of the scent that reminded her so much of Granny's. Moisture gathered in her eyes as she was flooded with more memories.

It occurred to her that Granny was notorious for leaving the key inside her car, as were most folks in town. Kelsey might not be able to walk away from the hospital but she could get that ankle to work well enough to press a gas pedal.

The thought of stealing, of adding to her list of crimes, caused another twinge of guilt.

Survival meant borrowing from others and working in the gray area of the morals she'd been taught as a youngster. Morals that she'd compromised out of desperation. It didn't matter that she'd been backed against a wall. She should have known what was happening when she agreed to be a courier for the customer she met at her nighttime drink slinging job on Harry Hines Boulevard. It was her responsibility to know.

Except the ladies she worked with said it was fine and that she was lucky to have been picked. They'd said almost everyone had 'run an errand' for a regular at some point for a wad of cash—cash that could dig her out of the financial hole that was crippling her.

A dark figure came running past as a male voice shouted, "Hey!" from a different direction. The voice belonged to Kellan. But who was he shouting at?

Kelsey had two choices. She could slink down into the floorboard and pray he didn't know where she was. Or she could pre-empt and slide out with her hands up. Was Kellan alone or did the sheriff come out with him? Could she risk a glance?

The thought of someone running through the parking lot at this hour tightened the knot in her chest.

Before she could sit up, Kellan came into view. The door opened.

"Who does this belong to?" he asked, his gaze bouncing from her to the person who'd run by.

Fear shot through her as she realized she'd been found once again.

"I don't know," she admitted.

"Have you checked for a key fob inside the vehicle?" he asked.

"No. I was about to, though," she stated as she pulled herself up. "Who was that?"

"I didn't get a good look but I'm guessing he knows who you are," Kellan said, slipping into the driver's seat. He opened the console. "Bingo. Key fob, which means I could have pressed the button and we would have been fine.

"Go, hurry, please," she pleaded as the sheriff came running out of the glass doors.

Kellan dropped the key inside the cup holder on the console. "Tell me why I should drive off when the sheriff is looking for you."

More of that panic surfaced. Kellan was strong-willed too and just as stubborn as she could be.

"I will if you get us out of here," she said, sliding down in the backseat.

"As soon as I turn my back, you'll run again," he pointed out.

"I give you my word, Kellan. Please."

The sheriff stepped off the curb. She ducked.

"But we have to go now or he'll catch us," she said. She'd been purposefully ambiguous. Kellan could decide for himself which 'he' she was talking about. "My life is in danger, Kellan."

His gaze studied her from the rearview mirror but he didn't budge.

"I did something bad and now I'm trapped," she admitted. "If I go to jail, they'll find me in my cell. It'll be made to look like I did it to myself and my mother will be all alone."

The sheriff crossed the internal street that looped around the hospital, heading in their direction.

"You've already seen what one person is capable of doing to me," she pleaded. "The equipment shed. He won't stop until he gets what he wants or I'm dead. Or both."

"Sounds like the law is the only thing that can help you," Kellan stated. He lifted his right hand and let his finger hover in front of the button that would start the engine.

"Would you believe me if I said the law is the last place I can safely go?"

5

Kellan didn't hide. For one, he wasn't a criminal and refused to act like one. However, curiosity was getting the best of him about Kelsey's situation. Whoever she was talking about had come close to ending Kellan's life, making it personal for him too.

So, he pushed the button to start the engine.

A vehicle pulling out of the lot at this hour while everyone searched for Kelsey would draw attention. "My cell phone is on Firebrand property, not that far from my house."

"Is going there a mistake?" Kelsey asked. He understood her concern.

"We might not make it out of this parking lot," he said, releasing some of the pent-up frustration in a near-hiss.

Kellan exhaled a sharp sigh as he thought about options, providing they did make it out of the area. They'd just stolen a vehicle. Once he could safely get to a phone, he would have a car waiting for the owner of this vehicle. He could check the glovebox for the owner's name. There was normally an insurance card or service record kept there.

Bronc Harris, the ranch foreman, would be able to handle ensuring the owner had a replacement until the vehicle could be returned. Or, better yet, the family attorney. Since it was parked in the ER, he might not have a lot of time before the owner needed it back.

Kelsey didn't have a phone either or she would have made a call for help in the equipment shed. Going back to her vehicle was a risk he didn't want to take. All manner of thoughts ran through his head, not the least of which cast him as a criminal just like his mother. Even though he was helping someone, his recent actions weren't legal. Kellan could try to convince himself that he was doing nothing more than borrowing a car instead of theft. But that was just rationalizing on his part. Trying to soften his crime.

The drive away from the hospital was the longest few minutes of his life. At this time of night, there were no other vehicles on the road. But they made it off the lot without a roadblock or host of sirens heading their way.

They would stick out like a sore thumb if he didn't get on the highway soon.

But go where?

Could they find a place to stop off, park the Taurus in a hidden spot, and get a few hours of sleep?

"I'm sorry that I dragged you into this, Kellan," Kesley finally said from the backseat. "You don't deserve this. Find a spot and drop me off. I'll tell the sheriff or whoever that I forced you to take the car."

"Forced me how?" he asked. There was no answer that made sense.

"I'll say that I had a gun," she said, clearly spitballing.

"That will only get you in deeper trouble," he countered.

"The kind of trouble I'm in can't get any deeper," she said on an exhale. Her shoulders slumped forward. "I want to tell you everything but I'm afraid the more you know, the more of a target you'll become."

"You and I escaped a burning shed on my property and we made the decision to steal a car." He doubted he could get in any thicker than that.

"Well, then, you have to leave town." She glanced around like there was something magic in the vehicle that could transport him somewhere else. "Leave the country. Give it time to die down and then come back once it's all settled." The next exhale caused air to deflate out of her lungs similar to air being let out of a balloon. "You're a Firebrand. You have enough money to hide until it's safe to return."

"What will you do?" he asked.

"At some point, this is going to catch up to me," she said. "I got involved with the wrong people. They have connections. I was naïve to think I could come back here for my father's funeral one last…"

She seemed to catch herself.

Since he didn't assume she meant to harm herself, he figured she intended to disappear. Was coming home more about seeing her mother one last time?

"What will the law find in your car?" he asked.

"My cell, cash, ID," she admitted.

He glanced at the rearview mirror, saw a flash in her eyes. Something clicked.

Of course, she would want to get to her cell and money, not to mention her wallet. But there was something else brewing based on the desperation in her tone. "And who will they think you are?"

Kelsey bit down on her bottom lip.

"You promised answers, Kelsey." By some miracle, they made it onto the highway. "I have no idea how long we get a free pass in this vehicle. Someone is going to notice it's missing and report it."

After a sharp sigh, she began, "I already said that I got mixed up in something that I shouldn't have. You have to understand how desperate I was, or there's no way I would have agreed."

"Understood." Kellan didn't like the sound of this. He pulled off the highway and onto a side road that led to one of his favorite fishing holes. They could park in the trees and figure out their next steps.

His mind also snapped to his mother's situation. She'd become desperate to get more than their fair share of money from the Marshal. She'd tried to get close to him, tried to persuade him to change the will and give her side of the family more of the pie. To make a long story short, that failed, a new person swooped in after the Marshal's death, claiming rights to some of the inheritance, and Jackie Firebrand attempted to murder her.

His patience for desperate acts ran thin.

Once he found a good spot to park, he cut off the engine and turned toward the backseat. "Keep going because you haven't told me anything yet."

"I'm guessing you want more than generalities."

Kellan grunted. "My life is now on the line too. You're telling me to run away from my home for an undetermined period of time. I think I deserve answers, Kelsey."

"Fair points," she said, then pleaded with her eyes. "It's just there's a point of no return in every situation. You know?"

His patience was beginning to run thin. "Last I checked, we're past it now that I've stolen a car for you."

Kelsey stared him in the eyes. An inconvenient jolt of

electricity shot through him, sending warmth to places that didn't need to be active right now.

"Be prepared to see me in a different light, Kellan."

Was that the real reason she stalled? She was ashamed of something she'd done?

"Whatever else you're about to say, I know you're a good person underneath it all and wouldn't hurt a soul," he said to reassure her.

"Easy to say from where you're sitting," she continued. "Back here, the picture isn't so pretty."

"Start at the beginning, then, and tell me everything," he said. Aside from the obvious reasons of the two of them being criminals at this point, he wanted to know how a kind, gentle soul like Kelsey could end up running from the law.

She shook her head. "The rest is too embarrassing to admit. I'll give you the high level of who is after me and why."

Sounded like a good place to start.

"When you remember me, though, what do you think?" she asked, surprising him by turning the tables.

"That you've always been beautiful inside and out," he said, clearing the sudden dryness in his throat with a cough.

The compliment had the opposite of its intended effect. Instead of smiling, she frowned and cast her eyes down at the floorboard.

"See," she said. "I tell you what I've gotten myself into and I lose that forever."

"Try me," he said, moving into the backseat with her.

She scooted over to make room for him.

"Trust me?" he asked, but it was more of a request than a question.

~

KELSEY REALIZED she was hemming and hawing. It was so nice to have someone look at her like she was the old Kelsey again, even if she knew it wouldn't last. Kellan deserved to know the truth. The look in his eyes said she could trust him. Why was it so hard to trust *anyone* anymore?

A noise outside the car startled her. She brought her hand up to cover a gasp.

Kellan immediately jumped into action, holding a finger up to his lips, indicating they should both be very still, very quiet.

It had to be the middle of the night at this point. They were parked off the gravel road he'd turned onto. Who would be out here?

Kelsey's first thought was the bastard found her again. How? They hadn't left a trail. No one had followed them from the hospital parking lot, much to her surprise and, she was certain, to Kellan's.

There were plenty of deer in these parts. Wild hogs too. She should know. She'd almost lost a hand to an angry one. In the nick of time, a hunter had come along, shooting the hog and saving the day. Her luck had run out a long time ago. If the same scenario happened today, she could kiss her hand goodbye.

Kelsey's eyes had adjusted to the dark. She definitely saw motion in the thicket about twenty feet from the vehicle.

At this point, they were sitting ducks if that was a person. If it was law enforcement, she wouldn't fare much better. One meant to take her life and the other would send her to prison. Both choices were awful. Both meant they would get to her. But then, constantly running wasn't exactly a life.

And to what end?

When would it stop? When she was behind bars or

dead? Handing over the contents of what she'd been asked to deliver?

The last one was laughable because she would definitely be dead if she handed over the 'product' as it had been called.

The flash of light over in the trees nearly stopped her heart. A phone app? A flashlight?

"Go along with me, okay?" Kellan asked as the light flashed again, moving closer.

She leaned away from him.

"Trust me?" he asked. There was that question again. "Never mind. I know you do or you wouldn't have shown up on Firebrand land."

A few arguments against it sprung to mind but this wasn't the time to push back. Instead, she gave a slight nod.

Kellan closed the distance between them in the car, braced himself with one hand on the floorboard and the other cupping her face, and then kissed her.

The moment his lips met hers, her heart free fell. If she'd been standing, her legs would have given out, her bones melted. Now, she finally understood what going weak at the knees meant. She'd never experienced it before. But then, it had been a very long time since she'd been kissed at all.

Jackson had left a bitter taste in her mouth for getting close enough to anyone for kissing. He'd ruined her for trusting men. He'd ruined her for relationships. And he'd ruined her for believing she had a future.

But for a split-second, she believed she could have everything with a man like Kellan. The kind of love that caused her stomach to tingle when he was near. The kind of love that would give her room to fly, to chase her dreams. The kind of love that made her ready to come home every night, stay up late talking, and have more sex in a month than she'd had in a year while married.

"Hey," a male voice said as the flashlight beam threatened to blind her once Kellan shifted. The air was immediately cold without his warmth.

An older dude knocked on the window like this was a police raid. She should know. She'd heard plenty of them over the years.

Kellan held up a hand to stop the man from blinding them. He cracked the door open and stepped outside. She noticed that he managed to block most of her face from prying eyes as he leaned against the door.

"My apologies," Kellan said. "My girlfriend and I got a little carried away."

"Motel's on the highway," the older man said, disapproval in his tone. She knew that tone a little too well too. "No reason to be out here doing the devil knows what."

Kelsey opened her mouth to defend them, but it dawned on her that it was best if this person believed they were making out. She wanted to point out that they were both in their late thirties and consenting adults.

The argument died on her lips. The less this man questioned, the better for all involved.

"My bad," Kellan said, keeping a cool head. She recalled that he once had a temper but then a lot had most likely changed in the years she'd been away. "We'll get off your property immediately, sir."

Good for Kellan, because a piece of Kelsey was fuming.

"Aren't you one of those Firebrand boys?" the man asked.

"You must have me confused with someone else," Kellan said, turning his face away from the light. He put a hand up to block the beam.

The older man was being a jerk.

"Is that right?" the man asked. "Because I could swear you look just like one of 'em."

"I better get my car off your property and head home," Kellan said, redirecting the conversation.

"Don't come back here in the middle of the night," the man warned. "Next time, I won't be so forgiving."

Forgiveness?

Kelsey had to bite her tongue before she spouted something she would regret. Last she checked, being mean to strangers wasn't exactly considered biblical. The interaction reminded her that Kellan was recognizable. And, honestly, she might be too.

If anyone realized who she was, they would likely call up her mother. Gossips were also nosy as it turned out. Kelsey couldn't afford for her mother to find out that she'd come into town without so much as a word, as much as she'd wanted to see her mother again before she disappeared. She would be Anne Stepford after that, with the fake ID the bouncer at the strip club had arranged for a small fee. Dale had been a lifesaver. He'd warned her about the ID, though. Said to be careful with it.

Disappearing across the Mexican border had seemed like a good idea. On the way there, she'd made a pitstop here in Lone Star Pass. She'd arranged for a storage unit on the outskirts of town and had deposited the 'product' in one of the air-conditioned rooms.

Once she crossed the border, that's where her plan started falling apart. She had no place to go, figuring she would cross that bridge when she came to it.

The thought of leaving her mother alone to care for herself as she got older had gutted Kelsey, once she saw how her mother had aged. She'd seen occasional pictures on social media posted from someone in the congregation. Her mother never posted anything. She didn't even have a personal social media page. Just the one for the church.

The first couple of years, Kelsey barely looked back. Too hurt to come home and too stubborn to admit her mistake.

Maybe there was more of her father in her than she wanted to admit.

Now that he was gone, regret filled her for the fact they'd never been able to make things right between them. Time had run out. Neither could apologize or tell the other person they loved them. Would the same happen with her mother?

Regret caused moisture to pool in her eyes. She wiped it away. Open the floodgates and they might never close again. At almost thirty-nine years old, she'd already amassed a lifetime of regret. And now, if she wasn't careful, she could spend the rest of her life in prison.

6

Kellan took the driver's seat, turned on the car, and banged a U-turn. He couldn't get away from the older gentleman fast enough.

Thankfully, the man hadn't taken a picture of the license plate. The older dude had been just suspicious and grouchy enough to do something like that. Who needed Neighborhood Watch with a guy like that around?

Kellan's mistake was that he didn't realize there were cabins in this area. With a location off the highway and this being a popular fishing spot, he should have known it would have been developed at some point. It had been years since he'd gone off ranch property to fish since he rarely took a day off. Constant fighting within the family took a toll and made him feel like he had to be working at all times.

Toward the end of the lane that would dump him off onto the service road, he'd missed the small sign for the development. As it happened, he could turn left to find the model cabin. A model cabin would be empty until morning.

This area must not get much traffic since the old man heard the car coming up the gravel lane. They needed a place to rest and hide out for a little while. Maybe even find a phone.

He pulled up to the model that was situated next to the lake. He'd be damned. Stand still long enough and the world would change around you.

"I doubt anyone's here in the middle of the night," he said to Kelsey. "We should be able to get some rest."

"There's no way I could sleep after what just happened," Kelsey said, even though she bit back a yawn. The body decided when it needed rest.

"It'll get us out of the elements and this car, which might have been reported as stolen already," he pointed out. There was still no phone available. Would the model have a landline installed?

Somehow, he doubted it.

He didn't know a soul who still used a home phone, but he had a bigger problem. Was there an alarm system?

Out here, there was a solid chance the builder didn't put an alarm system into the model. If he did, it was unlikely to be armed. There were exceptions, of course. If the builder stored any valuables inside, they might have one installed and armed. He pulled up to the cabin and cut his lights. The small parking area led to a beautiful log cabin that looked designed for weekend getaways.

Kellan turned off the engine. "I'll be right back."

Kelsey sat up, eyes wide. She bit back another yawn, clearly fighting sleep. She had to be overclocked at this point. He needed to get her to a place where she could catch at least a couple hours of sleep. A shower would do wonders. If there was a washer, he could give her clean clothes.

When everything was stripped from you, those basic

things that you take for granted suddenly become everything.

After walking the perimeter of the home, he deemed it safe to go inside. It would be a shame to break glass, so he checked each door and window. Hit paydirt with the master bedroom. The opening was good size. Even someone with his height would fit. Although, to be fair, he could hoist Kelsey inside first. Then, she could walk to one of the doors and let him in.

But physical contact was a bad idea. Best avoided unless absolutely necessary. Every time he touched Kelsey, a coil tightened in his chest. The kiss, as benign as it had been meant to be, had felt downright erotic, despite being a show for the older man. Kellan had to give it to the senior, though; he was ready to protect his land with a cell phone in one hand and a shotgun dangling out of the other arm.

"We're good," he said to Kelsey, returning to the car. By his calculations, they had by morning at the latest before the Taurus would be reported stolen. It would be fantastic if he could get the vehicle back to the lot. Since that wasn't looking realistic, the best he could hope was to get word back. He'd almost been desperate enough to ask to borrow the older gentleman's phone. Of course, that would have given a whole host of other headaches to deal with, and he was beyond his quotient for one evening.

Kelsey exited the vehicle and then followed him around to the side where the master bedroom waited. He'd already opened the window, so he clasped his hands together to give her a boost up.

She planted one hand on his shoulder and the other on the sill. A few seconds later, she was in.

It occurred to him a worker might drop by first thing in the morning. He planned to be long gone, but if someone beat him to the punch, he didn't want to give away the fact they were inside. Plus, a vehicle with no occupants would draw too much unwanted attention. "I better hide the car, just to be safe."

"I'll unlock the front door for you and then head to the shower," Kelsey said, her voice beginning to sound normal again. He took it as a good sign she was healing on her own.

The image of her naked in the shower tightened the coil in his chest. Kellan forced it from his thoughts as he parked the car behind a wall of shrubs meant to cordon off the property line. Next door to the model, a cabin was mid-construction. A few plots over, another was in the early stages of being prepped. The foundation had been poured. All of these butted up to the lake. The entrances were toward the small lot, which would allow for patios that faced the lake.

Kellan had mixed feelings.

Progress was good. Bringing weekenders to the area would be good for the local economy. Still, a piece of him—and it was the piece that kept him at Firebrand Cattle, despite all the fighting and challenges that came along with working with and for family—wished the area could be left alone.

After hiding the car, he joined Kelsey inside the cabin and locked the door behind him. She'd kept the lights on dim, which was smart. It wasn't completely dark inside, but he couldn't see that the lights were on from the outside when the blinds were closed either. A win-win if ever he saw one.

The cabin was decorated in a fancy manner, with a leather couch in front of a stone fireplace. Two chairs and a decent-sized square coffee table rounded out the room. Every board game known to man, along with an array of paperback novels, filled the bookcase next to the fireplace. He'd never understood placing books next to a fire but it made for a nice aesthetic. As long as the fireplace was gas, it would work alright, he guessed. Gas fireplaces didn't burn as hot or put out as much heat. The pages and cardboard boxes should be safe instead of tinder.

Even so, if he'd been the builder—maybe it was the rancher in him talking—he wouldn't put tinder anywhere near a fireplace.

The cabin was cozy and otherwise well-designed. The galley-style kitchen had all the latest appliances in stainless steel. The counters were made of granite. The cabinets painted white, which made the area feel bigger than it was.

There was a working coffee machine. Hallelujah! And pods.

He checked the fridge and found some leftover pizza, along with milk he assumed was meant to be used as creamer. And pre-made cookie dough that he guessed was for visitors. Make the kids happy, give a family feel to the place, and make a sale. Sounded plausible to him.

Everything else was fake. There was plastic cereal in a clear container on top of the counter. A bowl of fake limes sat on the counter as well. It made sense but, damn, he was hoping to hit paydirt with something edible.

Inside the pantry, he found stacks of bottled water. They could use those. He grabbed a couple, and then downed one. The IV at the hospital had rehydrated him enough to keep him up and running. This was for good measure.

Plus, if they needed to take to the woods to camp for a few days, he needed to stock up.

Would it come to that?

Camping? Running?

At this point, he was just trying to get through the next couple of hours without being shot at or arrested.

And without kissing Kelsey again.

~

Kelsey turned off the spigot. She quickly dried off and then searched for a robe or something she could use to cover more skin. After the kiss in the car, she didn't need to feel any more exposed to Kellan than she already did.

The kiss had burned all the way down to her toes. As much as she didn't like the idea of comparisons, Jackson was the only other person she'd kissed. There was no comparison between the two. Kellan was dozens of fires lighting inside her at the same time as butterflies launched in her chest. He was heat and passion and what a kiss should feel like when you committed yourself to a person.

She'd missed out on so much, even though she knew on instinct this was not the norm.

If she ever found another person that gave her those same butterflies, while making her feel safe, she would consider a relationship.

Would she though?

Kelsey took a good, hard look in the mirror. She'd never wanted to start a family with Jackson, believing far too long that something was broken inside of her because of it. She was beginning to separate out the idea that she didn't want a family with that she didn't want a family *with Jackson*. The idea of kids with someone like Kellan was a different ballgame.

What if it had been him who'd asked her out all those years ago? How different would her life have turned out?

For one, she would be a mother by now. Of that, she was

certain. For another, she would have had great sex, considering the heat in the kiss they'd shared. Of that, she was also certain. Would she live at Firebrand? Would she have lost herself in the same way she had marrying Jackson?

It was only now that Kelsey was beginning to think she might have a shot at a future. It was the reason she'd agreed to run the errand despite knowing it was wrong. When the easy way out of her situation had presented itself, she'd taken it. What did that say about her character?

Kellan looked at her with eyes of appreciation, like he was staring at something unique and beautiful. She didn't deserve it. Not after the life she'd led. And he needed to know the truth. Because if he kept looking at her with those eyes, she would give in to the burning ache growing inside her chest and ask him for something she shouldn't want…him.

The liquid soap at the bathroom sink had sufficed for shampoo and body wash. However, the lack of toothpaste and toothbrush was a problem.

Opening and closing drawers, she scored bigtime on the last one. Toothpaste.

After finger-brushing her teeth, which was better than nothing, she located a white cotton bathrobe. Bundling up her clothes, she entered the kitchen where she smelled coffee brewing. The coffee was almost too good to be true.

"Hey," she said before entering, so she wouldn't startle Kellan. He chased dangerous poachers, tracking them down and then sitting on them until law enforcement arrived. Even as a teenager, the Firebrands had a reputation for being good at dealing with dangerous people. Had she instinctively come to their property? Because she didn't remember making a conscious choice after picking up a tail on the way home from visiting her father's grave.

Kellan turned to face her. A flash of something—need?—crossed his features. It was only a split second but unmistakable.

"You should get some rest," he said, his voice low and gravelly. Sexy.

She couldn't continue deceiving him.

"We need to talk, Kellan."

He cocked an eyebrow.

"Coffee sounds great," she said to him. "Is there enough for two cups?"

He poured a second one before handing it over along with a bottle of water. Then, he motioned toward the round four-seat table in the adjacent room.

Kelsey glanced around after shoving the bundle of dirty clothes into one of the bags she'd been given. She took down a bottle of water next. She then gripped the mug with both hands, rolling it around for warmth as she searched for the right words to say. "The windows here in the corner are nice."

"Yes," he agreed.

"And the fireplace is loaded with games and books. I can see where this would be a great weekend getaway for a family," she said, hemming and hawing.

"Same," he said before taking a sip. This was the second one-word answer in a matter of seconds.

Staring at the coffee rim instead of his beautiful eyes helped drum up enough courage to say what she needed to. "I'm not a saint, Kellan. I've done a lot of bad things."

"No one is," he said matter-of-factly. He had no idea. The man probably assumed she'd given the grocery store cashier expired coupons or something simple like that.

Newsflash. This was not small. This fell into the 'huge and awful things' category.

"I know," she said, shifting in her seat. "What I'm about to tell you can't leave this room. It would kill my mother if it got back to her."

"You have my word," he said. His attention too because he leaned toward her.

"Please don't hate me," she continued, unable to meet his eyes. "Once Jackson and I married, I didn't want to sit at home all day so I got a job as a barista."

So far, so good.

She could keep going.

"We moved around so much that I never had a chance to go to school or stay at a job for more than a year," she continued, focusing on one word at a time.

"I never heard much about his career, but then I'm probably the last to know most things," he said.

"It was promising at first," she said. "But I should back up. The reason I never came home is that my parents disowned me for marrying him in the first place."

"I'm sorry," he whispered. "Sounds right up the Marshal's alley." He paused. "It must have been difficult growing up under the scrutiny of being the pastor's daughter."

"It was," she admitted. "The fishbowl was bad." She risked a glance, caught his gaze, and her heart threatened to leap from her chest. "You would know a thing or two about that, wouldn't you?"

"That's correct," he said. "Not an easy life by any means."

"I was determined to make my marriage work," she said. "To prove to my parents that I'd made the right decision."

"Understandable."

"When you have a stubborn streak like mine, lines are crossed that probably shouldn't be," she said. "My pride wouldn't let me come back defeated, divorced."

"I'm learning there are worse things," he said.

"Sounds like you have experience."

"I'm divorced," he said on a sharp sigh.

Kelsey reached across the table and touched his hand. "I'm sorry, Kellan. I had no idea."

"Long story."

Aren't they all? "I'd still like to hear it sometime."

He nodded. "Another time. Right now, we're talking about you."

Right. "Okay." She took another breath. "I figured out my mistake in the first year but couldn't admit it, not even to myself until years later. Turns out hindsight gives near-perfect vision."

His eyebrow shot up. "How did you stick it out that long?"

"Didn't let myself focus on the bad," she said. "Plus, Jackson was gone most of the time anyway. I was basically living as a single person. I rarely called home and, when I did, convinced myself I was only telling my folks what they wanted to hear. That Jackson's music was taking off." She shrugged. "They loved it when I sang. They were big fans of music."

"I remember you singing at special services," he stated.

"I know lying to my parents sounds terrible, but it isn't even the worst part."

"Go on," he urged. "You can trust me."

Could she?

Because she wanted to.

She wanted to more than anything.

7

Kellan couldn't imagine much would shock him these days. He wanted to know more about what happened to Kelsey after she left town. The fact she could barely look him in the eye stabbed him in the chest. No decent person should have to carry around the kind of guilt and shame that made eye contact look like it created physical pain.

She bit down on her bottom lip, then took another sip of coffee before continuing.

"You can tell me anything, Kelsey. I promise I've done worse and made bigger mistakes," he said to reassure her.

Based on her expression, it didn't work.

Whatever it was, it looked like it weighed her down. She needed to get it off her chest. The only way to do that was to talk.

Patience. He needed to wait. She would get there. It was obvious she wanted to talk about it as much as she probably needed to.

"Right," she started again. "This is harder than I thought,

so I'm going to blurt it out and we can sort out the details later."

"Sounds good," he said. "Sometimes it's best to rip the proverbial Band-Aid."

"Here goes." She held up a finger before taking another sip of coffee. "Jackson cheated on me with a bandmate. He left me for her, in fact. Although, our marriage had been dead for so long I'm surprised it took as long as it did."

Patience. He nodded. Being cheated on hurt like hell.

"But that was recently," she said. "What I didn't know was that he'd been lying to our landlord and not paying rent. I gave him all the money. He insisted on being the one to handle finances because he wanted to ease my burden. He said one of his friends helped him get odd jobs so he could pitch in more financially." She flashed eyes at him. "You'd think I would have learned my lesson by then but he started showering every day, dressing nice again, and cutting back on drinking. I thought he was making a turnaround. Figured once we got back on our feet financially that we could discuss moving on, getting divorced."

"But he wasn't."

"No, he wasn't," she parroted. "Unbeknownst to me, he was also opening up charge accounts in both of our names, forging my signature."

"It's surprisingly easy to do this now," he interjected.

"Silly me, because I had no idea any of this was happening," she said. "I guess I built up this story in my head that if I stuck around long enough the marriage would somehow work out or we would divorce like civilized adults. The last thing I could do was come crawling home, begging for money or a place to live like my parents believed would happen. Not after what they said to me." Again, she shrugged. "I guess I didn't have a place to go, so I stayed. We were too broke for me to save anything to get my own apartment without his help."

Kellan wished he'd known. He could have helped her out. But he understood pride. His had nearly severed his relationship with his cousins, especially Corbin, for the rest of their lives. "People get cheated on and divorced, Kelsey. It sucks. But it doesn't make you a bad person. Broken maybe, but not bad."

"That's not the bad part, Kellan. I'm working up to that."

"Fair enough," he said.

"Here's the thing," she said. "I was in the hole financially. I had no way to get out. My landlord locked the doors and kept all my stuff once Jackson moved in with his girlfriend. A co-worker at the coffee shop where I worked took pity and lent me enough money to rent a pay-as-you-go motel. I couldn't wait for a paycheck if I wanted to eat. I was in Dallas in a not-so-great part of town and there was a bar I could walk to that needed waitresses."

He stopped himself from saying there was nothing wrong with making an honest living. The way Kelsey looked at him told him there was more to the story.

"Here I was, the shy kid, pastor's daughter who sang in church, and now I was signing up to serve drinks in a topless club in Dallas for tips so I could eat," she said with the biggest exhale he'd heard so far.

Rather than speak, he reached across the table and took her hand in his, giving a reassuring squeeze. He could see how working in a gentlemen's club could seem like the end of the world to someone as good-natured as Kelsey. She'd been brought up to believe everything was a sin, according to her father. The preacher was known for being strict. Hell, even the Marshal had commented once or twice on the rigid nature of the town's preacher. That was saying a whole helluva lot for a man who pitted his own sons together, had cheated on his wife, and generally was a bad human being. He'd run his own grandson out of town when he found out about him getting his girlfriend pregnant while still in high school.

Kelsey didn't withdraw her hand. He took it as a good sign that his touch reassured her when his words had failed miserably up to this point.

"Can you imagine if my parents would have found out about their daughter working in a strip club? Or anyone else in town, for that matter."

He gave a slight head shake.

"There's more," she said. "I was struggling but making ends meet. I wasn't making any progress on the debt and my credit rating dropped faster than a roller coaster on its first big hill. I didn't see a way out of the dangerous hellhole where I lived." She shrugged again. "I was deflated and tired from serving coffee four mornings a week and the club gave me three nights. During one of my shifts at the topless bar, I was approached by someone I knew better than to talk to. We didn't have stations. All waitresses worked the floor. We waited at the door in line like taxi cabs at the airport. When someone new came in and it was our turn, we got to walk the person or party to a table or booth and then take drink orders."

"Sounds like they had the system down," he commented.

"Have you been to one of those places, Kellan?"

He shook his head. "It's not because I'm self-righteous. The ranch has always kept me busy."

"Good," she said. "Don't go. I was literally stepping over things in the parking lot that were disgusting." She paused. "I guess some of the waitresses make a little extra money on the side going out to the parking lot with some of the clientele while on their breaks."

"Weren't there cops around to stop that behavior?" he asked.

"You'd be surprised at what goes on," she stated. "Dallas has a lot of crime that would shock you."

None of it would ever make sense to him, least of all not protecting the women working in establishments like those.

"Anyway, this guy asks me if I want to go outside one night," she continued. "I told him no and that I wasn't up for anything but serving drinks. But he grabs me by the wrist and orders shots. I'm surprised because he's alone but what I didn't realize is that he has someone outside in the parking lot, waiting. He sends a text and another guy walks in, insists on me walking him to his table. The door person tells him this establishment isn't a restaurant. But he says his friend is already inside so they flagged me down and sent me to the table where I put the first guy." She studied him as embarrassment flushed her cheeks. "This guy looks like the person who gets sent into a situation when someone doesn't pay up. But he asks me to run an errand for a big cash payout."

"And you agreed," he said without judgment.

"Not at this point," she said. "I couldn't figure out why on earth they wanted me to be the one to run this errand for them. I've never met these two a day in my life."

"Someone was behind the scenes? Pulling strings?"

"That's what I thought initially, but then I figured I must still look like the church girl who sits in the pews on Sunday," she continued. "No one would suspect me of doing anything illegal. I can't tell you how many of the club's clientele commented on how I didn't look like I belonged in a place like that."

"Desperation can make people do things that are out of character," he said, feeling like the biggest jerk. His mother had broken the law and could have killed someone. However, she didn't. She'd been caught. Her mind wasn't right due to past abuse that had warped her. And what had he done? Kick her when she was down instead of showing support.

That made him a jerk and a hypocrite.

"My neighbor in the rent-by-the-week motel stopped by to tell me goodbye one afternoon," she continued. "Said she ran an errand for someone where she worked and it turned out to be her ticket out. She described men just like the ones who asked me." More of that embarrassment burned but it only made her more beautiful. "Easy money became too great a temptation to pass up. The side job was going to give me a chance to start over, get out of the circumstances I was in. It was going to be my ticket out of working at the club. Every shift, I feared someone from back home would walk in and see me there."

Kellan leaned forward, close enough to feather a kiss on her lips. They tasted like a mix of peppermint and dark roast. "Making a mistake doesn't make you a bad person, Kelsey."

"Really? Because I always believed our choices define us."

There was an air of truth to that statement. One, he couldn't deny. One that made him just as big of a jerk as the next guy.

"No argument there," he admitted. Was he making a mistake getting close to Kelsey again?

∼

"All I could see was a way out of circumstances that had been defining me far too long," Kelsey admitted.

"I'm guessing you took the job from the men at the club," Kellan said.

"Yes. They gave me a box that was the size of a trunk. Told me not to open it. One of Jackson's friends had sold me an old van they used to drive around for gigs after he left me. I guess he felt sorry for me. Anyway, I was supposed to drive the box across the border and bury it. But I got cold feet," Kelsey said. "Couldn't go through with it. Call it a bout of morals."

"It's because you are still a good person who ended up in a bad situation," Kellan corrected.

As much as she appreciated him for trying to give her an out, she didn't deserve one. Her life sank to new lows.

"The guys who are after me have connections with the cops in Dallas too," she added. "That's why I couldn't go to them. Now, that the sheriff has my name and will file a report, I'm in deeper trouble because more will show up here."

"Did you go to the police originally?"

"No." She shook her head for emphasis.

"Then, how do you know they won't help you?"

"Would you risk it if you'd heard someone had friends in high places?" she asked before it dawned on her that Kellan did have a big last name. "Never mind. You, of all people, wouldn't understand." She erected a safety wall in between them. Had she said too much? Exposed herself? Did he despise her now?

"Am I running?" he asked defensively. Clearly, she'd struck a nerve.

"No."

"Am I looking at you differently?" His voice dropped an octave, like it did when he was angry.

She didn't risk a glance. Connecting with those eyes of his would distract her, make it even more difficult to tell him everything.

His hand came up to her chin and with the gentlest of touches, he tilted her face toward him until she had no choice but to find his eyes.

There was nothing but compassion in those gorgeous browns. They calmed places inside her she didn't deserve.

"For how long?" she finally asked.

"Always," he reassured.

As much as she longed to believe him and lean into his strength, she couldn't allow herself to get swept up into all that was Kellan.

"You just don't understand," she said.

"Don't I?" he asked. "I'm guessing you haven't heard about my mother then."

She cocked her head to one side. "What happened to Mrs. Firebrand?"

"She's in jail in Houston, awaiting trial for attempted murder," he said.

"I'm so sorry," she whispered. "I had no idea what was going on back home. But I'm sure the law will figure out she didn't—"

"That's where you're wrong, Kelsey. She is guilty as the day is long. She admitted to her crime. She is throwing herself on the court and begging for mercy." He gave her a rundown of the abuse his mother endured in her own home. He followed up with recounting sexual abuse she'd endured as a teen by an uncle and the fact her parents didn't believe her when she finally plucked up the courage to say something. How she became a trophy wife to his father and then drank every day to distance herself from children she thought she would ruin if she got too close to.

"I had no idea," Kelsey said to him, looking him straight in the eyes now, moisture gathering in hers. "I'm sorry for her past and I'm sorry you had to grow up never knowing the real reason your mother was distant. You never talked about it. That couldn't have been easy for you."

He shook his head.

"With a father who was so busy trying to outdo his own brother that he didn't have time for his kids, someone had to step up," Kellan stated. "I was the oldest, so I took on the responsibility. Hell if I didn't screw that up big time."

"You needed parental guidance," she pointed out, not ready to let him take the fall. "And you did the best you could."

"Wasn't good enough," he quipped. "And my temper didn't make matters any better. Then, as though taking the heavy-handed approach didn't already damage my relationships with my siblings and cousins, I fell for my cousin's best friend, married her, and then got my heart handed to me when she divorced me to marry him." He exhaled a slow breath. "Well, not exactly to marry him, but they are married now," he corrected.

"Would I sound like a hypocrite if I said you were doing the best you could after being dealt a crappy hand?" she asked as some of the crushing weight lifted from her chest.

"Ever notice how easy it is to dole out forgiveness to others when they've done nothing to hurt you?" he asked. "And so damn hard to give it to yourself?"

Kelsey glanced at the clock, avoiding that question like the plague. An hour and a half had passed by in a blink. "It's nearly five o'clock." Getting lost in conversation with Kellan was a little too easy. She could sit here in this little kitchen forever like this with him and be totally happy.

Clothing optional.

Rather than go down the road of wishing for things she could never have, she cleared her throat.

"Any food in the fridge?" she asked, thinking they needed to change the subject before getting back out there. The break from the cold and wind had been beyond amazing.

"Unfortunately not," Kellan supplied, not calling her out for the shift in conversation and mood.

Before they got too far off topic, she circled back to say, "Thank you, Kellan."

"For what?"

"Talking to me about you, not judging me for what I confessed about me, being here right now," she said. "The list doesn't stop there."

He waved a hand like it was nothing.

"You put your reputation on the line for me," she continued because she had no intention of letting him get away with acting like he wasn't making huge sacrifices for her right now. "You could be arrested."

Another thought crossed her mind. He could end up dead.

What was she doing putting an innocent person at risk? Making a common criminal out of a good person?

Kellan didn't deserve this. His kindness wouldn't allow him to walk away. Sticking with her could end up killing him. Literally.

This was Kelsey's problem. She had no intention of dragging an innocent person into her nightmare. But what did she intend to do about it?

8

"I'm here and I'm not going anywhere without you," Kellan reassured Kelsey. She had a detached look in her eyes now. One he didn't like. Getting close to Kelsey was like standing close to a campfire in the dead of winter. Warmth radiated from her. Until she brought up a wall, then it was like being thrust into a dark cave.

"Plus, we need to get to the bottom of who is really after you and who sent them," he said to her, hoping to put a crack in said wall at a minimum. "You don't have any names?"

"No," she admitted.

"What about going back to the club and asking?" It was a longshot she would agree but he went for it anyway.

She was already shaking her head before he finished his sentence. "Not an option if I want to stay alive. Plus, it would be too dangerous for you to ask around. Unless you want to get shot."

He shook his head. "You didn't get a good look at the person who ran you off the road. Is that still true?" Now that she'd been honest with him about her past, maybe she might remember a detail she'd been suppressing.

"He wore dark clothing and sunglasses," she said. "I couldn't tell you what color hair he had."

"I keep wondering how the person found you here in Lone Star Pass unless word about your father spread," he said.

"That's my guess, as well," she agreed. "It makes sense they might be watching my family in case I got scared and came back home."

"What did you do with the delivery, by the way?"

She made the move where she flashed her eyes at him again.

He put his hands in the air, palms out, surrender position. "I'm not trying to find out for personal gain here."

"Oh, no. That's not what I'm afraid of at all. If I trusted anyone with the information, it would be you."

Trust. That was an interesting word.

"Then, what?" he asked.

"Telling you puts you more at risk," she reasoned.

She made a good point, except that he was already in this thing up to his eyeballs. "Just so you know, I fully intend to see this through whether I know what you did with the box or not."

"You have family to think of, Kellan. Your mother needs you."

He cracked a small smile. "You need me."

"I'll only bring more trouble to your doorstep," she pointed out.

"Trouble is my middle name," he said with that same grin, wider this time. Then, he laughed.

"What's so funny?" she asked, tilting her head to one side.

"You trying to protect me when I can take care of myself," he stated.

"I don't deserve your help," she said with a small voice—a voice that didn't sound like Kelsey at all. She might have been shy back in the day, but that didn't mean she didn't believe in herself. Life had delivered pro-boxer-level blows, but he couldn't allow himself to believe it had delivered a knockout punch.

"Everyone deserves help," he countered. And since he'd already made up his mind to stand by his mother, he was no longer a hypocrite. The forgiving himself bit was still a work in progress but he could get there. Correction, *would* get there.

She shook her head.

"Do I deserve a second chance at marriage?" he asked, turning the tables to make his point. "Not that I want one, but do I deserve one?"

She opened her mouth to speak and then clamped it shut.

"Of course, you do," she said after a pause. "If anyone does, it's you, Kellan."

"Case closed," he said, glancing at the clock. Time flew by when he was with Kelsey.

"But I've been lying to the people I love," Kelsey countered. "Making up a fairy tale life of a good marriage and tours through Europe."

"I thought your parents disowned you," he pointed out.

"They did for the first few years," she admitted. "One Christmas I got lonely and texted my mom. We started texting after that, which was when I started the lies."

"Your parents probably suspected something," he said.

"Nope," she said. "They wanted to believe me so they didn't push when I couldn't come home. I sent them doctored pictures. What kind of a person does that, Kellan? Lies to their parents and creates a false reality because the real one you're living in is just the worst, saddest thing and you don't want to bring them down with you. Enough time passes and you miss them so much that you no longer care about the hurtful things said. You want them to be proud of you once the stubbornness wears off."

"You didn't deserve to live like that, Kelsey."

"I did, though," she said. "We make our own bed, right? Then, we're the ones who have to lie in it, for better or worse. Remember? That was the promise I made."

"You couldn't have known your husband was going to fail and take you down with him," he countered. "You couldn't have predicted that he would give up on the marriage before it ever got off the ground."

"His music always came first," she said. "Looking back, it's so clear."

"You were eighteen years old, Kelsey. Not much more than a child yourself despite tasting freedom for the first time. Young people make mistakes. Hell, I still make mistakes. What's my excuse?"

Kesley sat there, quiet.

"Don't be harder on yourself than you would be someone else," he said. "Because you extend your kindness to everyone around you. Don't give all of it away. Save some for you."

She cocked her head to the other side. "That's good advice. Is that how you got through your divorce?"

Kellan laughed. He couldn't help it. "Hell, no. I'm still licking those wounds but talking this out with you makes me realize that I need to get over it and move on. Go back and apologize to those I hurt in the process."

She smiled too. It was like angels singing.

"So much easier to give advice than to take it, right?" she asked, but the question was rhetorical.

"Much easier," he agreed anyway before circling back to the problem at hand. They could get caught if they stuck around. "Businesses open up early around here, so we should probably head out as soon as possible. Don't want to be found squatting."

"Good point." Kelsey stood up. The bathrobe tie loosened. She caught it in time before the robe opened. Her cheeks turned six shades of red before she excused herself, mumbling something about getting dressed.

Heat flooded Kellan. The knot in his chest tightened as his fingers itched to run their tips along her silky skin. His throat suddenly dried up faster than Texas soil in the middle of August during a heat wave.

The question of where they should go couldn't be put off any longer, so he did his best to shake off the overwhelming need trying to take hold. Need for Kelsey. Need to take her in his arms. Need to touch her bare-naked skin.

Since going down that mental road wasn't productive, Kellan grabbed a couple of water bottles before cleaning up any trace someone had been there. He wiped down the counter, washed his cup, and then used the facilities. He had no idea how long it would be before he could use a proper bathroom again.

Hiding in the woods, camping, might keep them out of harm's way but how would they figure out who was behind the threat to Kelsey that way?

Was there some way he could signal to Bronc or one of his siblings that he needed transportation and cash? Clothes would be nice too but he wouldn't push his luck there. The fact he was hiding from the law after breaking it wasn't lost on him. He was of sound mind and body too, unlike his mother. Once this was over, he intended to apologize for the lack of support. Hell, the condemnation he'd bestowed on his fragile mother didn't exactly paint him in a good light. It occurred to him that he'd never be able to forgive his own screwups if he didn't learn how to forgive others for theirs.

Damn. He was getting deep.

For now, it was a tough enough job to figure out how to get Kelsey out of this dangerous situation in one piece.

There was no landline to use. A laptop sat on a desk but he wasn't a computer hacker so he didn't figure he could get past the initial startup screen without a password.

The sound of gravel crunching underneath tires got him moving. Kellan made a beeline to the master bathroom, where a wide-eyed Kelsey was slipping into her socks.

Neither spoke. Neither had to.

He nodded toward the window in the master before giving her an arm to lean on. Her dominant side ankle was either broken or sprained. Movement caused her to wince. At least it was wrapped. He would ask about that later. She had no shoes and a quick scan said there weren't any in the bedroom. He could have guessed but had learned a long time ago to check anyway.

The two were out the window as the front door opened. Shit.

Kellan realized he'd only washed out one cup...habit? Probably. He'd been a party of one most of his life. Some might say pity-party of one since his divorce but dating hadn't exactly topped the list of things he wanted to dive right into after being gutted by his marriage dissolving.

Talking to Kelsey about it eased the pain in a host of unexpected ways—ways he could dissect later when he wasn't about to scare the living daylights out of an innocent worker, probably get arrested, and who knew what else disaster awaited.

As they made a mad dash for the tree line, Kelsey stopped cold. "The key fob. We left them sitting on the table. They'll know someone has been here. Possibly find the car and then call the law."

Dread settled over Kellan like a heavy, wet cloak. She was right. They couldn't risk it. If the law was brought in now, they would link the stolen vehicle to him. Sheriff Lawler, who'd been good to Kellan, would know the two of them had been in this area. Considering the shape Kelsey was in, the sheriff would assume they wouldn't be able to go far. All he had to do was knock on the old man's door to learn who'd been driving the vehicle, even if the sheriff was giving Kellan the benefit of the doubt.

It was an impossible situation.

"Let's turn around, walk in the front door, then I need you to follow my lead," Kelsey said with determination.

At least one of them had a plan. For all Kellan's faults, he'd never been a liar. Never intended to be one either.

He could only hope the sheriff would understand once the two were able to sit down and have a conversation about everything that had gone down.

Could Kellan avoid jail time?

He had a feeling he was about to find out.

︴

KELSEY WAS ready to put all the lies behind her. So, her stomach churned at the thought of telling more. All she could do was find a shred of truth in whatever she was about to say to the worker, distract them, so Kellan could locate the fob.

Otherwise, his fingerprints were all over the fob. He would go down for auto theft. And she would never forgive herself.

Get the fob and she could wipe his prints clean. She could tell him that she wanted to hold onto the fob so they could return it to the rightful owner. And she would put her fingerprints all over it.

"Front door?" he asked like he wasn't too sure this was a good idea.

"It'll throw them off guard, but also they'll expect new clients to use the front," she said.

"We're clients now?"

"That's right," she said. "We'll figure out a backstory on the fly. Fair warning, I'm going to be as honest as possible."

"Okay," he said as he helped her up the front steps onto the small porch. "Do you know what you're going to say?"

She shook her head. "It'll come to me."

"You have no shoes," he pointed out.

"I got this," she reassured.

"Alright then," he said, opening the unlocked door.

"Hello?" Kelsey called out, figuring a woman's voice would be more reassuring than a man's if someone was caught off guard.

"Come in," a perky voice called back. "I'm just putting on a pot of coffee."

A young thirty-something blonde came bounding into the living room to greet them. She looked them up and down but smiled through her trepidation. "Early birds. I love it. Please. Come in and tell me a little about what brings you here this morning."

Kelsey tried to think of what she was going to say. She'd never been good at coming up with excuses on the fly because she'd always had time to craft a story. She smiled as she leaned on Kellan. "Mind if I sit at the table?"

"No, go right ahead," the bleached blonde with blue eye shadow and long, thick lashes said. There was suspicion in her voice so Kelsey needed to think fast.

"My-uh boyfriend and I were camping on the other side of the lake and I tripped on a rock as I got up to go to the bathroom," Kelsey said, hating the lie.

"Oh no," the woman said with dramatic flair. A frown settled on her features when she realized she wasn't about to get a sale. "Please. Sit down. My name is Avery."

Stick to as much truth as possible, Kelsey reminded herself. "I'm Kelsey and this is Kellan."

Avery looked Kellan up and down. "You look familiar. Have I seen you before?"

"Maybe at the lake, fishing," he offered, deflecting.

"That must be it," Avery bopped around the corner to the kitchen while they took seats at the kitchen table. "Coffee?"

"We're fine," Kelsey said. "Thank you, though." She needed to add more details to make her story believable as to why they'd shown up. "My boyfriend made ours over a campfire this morning."

"I had a guy do that for me once," Avery said from the other room. "I was spitting out coffee grinds for days." She laughed.

"That's a problem," Kelsey agreed, grabbing the fob before Kellan could swipe it as they sat down. She quickly tucked it in the pocket of her jeans after ensuring her fingerprints were all over it, covering any left behind by Kellan.

"Camping explains why I didn't hear you drive up," Avery said, joining them with a fresh mug in her hands.

"We actually walked around the lake yesterday and saw

this cabin, so we planned to come back and ask questions today anyway," Kelsey said.

Avery perked up big time.

"That right?" she asked, joining them at the table. "I have a book somewhere around here." She made a show of glancing around. "Don't forget to sign it before you leave, if we find it."

"Okay," Kelsey said. Now, she just needed to ask enough questions for them to be able to leave without drawing more unwanted attention. Avery would be able to give a description of them if the vehicle was somehow tracked here or found by one of the other residents. "Do some folks live here full time?"

"Most come up for weekends but we have a couple who love it so much they made it their primary home," Avery supplied. The cup sat in front of her. Both of her hands splayed out on the table, palms flat against the wood. "This place is truly magical with the lake views from your dining table. Did you see the patios?"

"We did," Kelsey said.

"Aren't they to die for?" Avery asked.

That was certainly one way to put it. "The sunsets must be amazing."

Avery leaned forward, her ample breasts resting on the tabletop. "Okay? Here's what I want you to think about." Her gaze bounced from Kellan to Kelsey and back. "You're sitting out on the back porch with a glass of wine just as the sun sets. The bright yellow-orange glow cast over the lake." She winked at Kelsey. "Maybe a kid or two running around, skipping rocks over at the lake."

"Sounds like a dream," Kelsey said, trying to come up with an exit plan before Avery got too into this scenario.

The saleswoman's cell rang in the other room.

She perked up. "I should probably take that. Cash gets worried if I don't answer when he calls. He worries about me opening up. Being out here alone so early. Do you mind?"

"Not at all," Kelsey said as Kellan reached for her hand across the table. His touch sent warmth through her. "We understand."

Kellan leaned over and feathered a kiss on Kelsey's lips—a kiss that practically sent sparks flying the moment their lips touched.

He held a certain magic that she might never find again.

But then, she'd have to learn to trust all over again in order to even consider the possibility of another relationship. After spending years in a relationship that made her feel lonelier than she could ever imagine, she'd talked herself out of falling down that rabbit hole again.

How different would her life be if she could allow herself to trust someone like Kellan?

Avery excused herself, grabbed her cell, and then carried on a full-on conversation while they sat there. Kellan squeezed Kelsey's hand, which gave her the courage to keep up the lie. In truth, though, she could see herself coming to a place like this with someone like Kellan. The kids might be a stretch. Kelsey's dreams of becoming a mother someday died alongside her ideals of marriage.

Not everyone got the whole package, she decided. So, she'd convinced herself that she didn't want those things.

Being with Kellan was opening her eyes to new possibilities.

With him?

9

Kellan sat back and watched as Kelsey took the lead, a master at work. For all these years he'd let himself believe her life had turned out to be as amazing as she deserved. Wasn't the truth always harder to swallow?

"Oh, is that right?" Avery said into the phone. The note of alarm in her voice caused him to sit up a little straighter. "Right from the parking lot?" She paused. "I'll lock my doors right now."

Kelsey caught Kellan's gaze and held it. The zing of electricity was more of a comfort than a surprise at this point.

"Okay, then," Avery said after they heard the click-click of her car being locked. "I've got clients in, so I'll have to call you back." Another pause. "Love you too."

Avery came back in the room with a tsk-tsk look on her face. "Can you believe someone stole a car from the ER parking lot?" She threw her hands up in the air. "People! Who can you trust these days?"

"That's awful," Kelsey said with a frog in her throat that could have given them away with a more astute person.

With a heavy sigh, Avery reclaimed her seat.

"Now, where were we?" she asked, the brightness returning to her eyes at the thought of a sale.

Kellan wanted to know more about the car theft. "What happened at the hospital is terrible. Do they have any suspects?"

Avery shook her head. "Ed, my husband, works in mechanical maintenance. All he said was to be sure to lock my car since there's a thief out running loose." She made a dramatic show of exhaling before straightening up again and locking gazes with Kesley. "Do we see bringing a family here someday?"

Kelsey cleared her throat. She glanced over at Kellan. "Yes. I think we do."

He nodded and smiled.

"Then, you'll want to lock a two-bedroom in now," Avery said. "They're selling the fastest."

All Kellan could think was how to get the hell out of there. News traveling about the car theft wasn't good. Would Sheriff Lawler assume Kelsey had taken it? He had to guess the two of them were together by now.

One thing in Kellan's favor was that he'd reported his cell phone as missing to the sheriff. Could he concoct a story that he couldn't reach the sheriff without his cell? That Kelsey had confided she didn't trust the law and begged for his help?

No, that would put her as the bad guy in this scenario. He wouldn't do that to her. Couldn't.

"Do you want a tour?" Avery asked.

"With my ankle, I should probably get back to camp," Kelsey said in a smooth move. "Do you have a brochure that we can take with us?"

"Um, sure," Avery said, sounding a little put off by the

request. She pushed up to standing before shaking her head. "I would just hate for you to miss out on one of these beauties." She sat back down and placed her palms on the table again. "How about this." She leaned in conspiratorially. "I can offer a ten percent off 'builder's special' on the pricing you'll see on the brochure. But you have to act today." She actually put her fingers in air quotes when she said the words *builder's special*. She lowered her voice to almost a whisper too. The tactic probably worked on a few people. He had to give it to Avery. She'd gotten what she thought was a bite and she pulled out all the stops to make a sale.

Kellan had a thought. Would it work?

He checked his pockets and made a face. "You know what? I must have left my cell back in my other pants." He mumbled a curse. "Mind if I use yours? I'd like to call my accountant to see what he thinks about putting down a deposit today."

Those words were like magic to Avery.

She practically hummed with excitement at the possibility of a sale.

"Let me grab it from the other room," she said with extra cheer in her voice. She rattled off details about the cabins, the plots available as she went into the kitchen.

Kellan lowered his voice to barely above a whisper and said, "Keep her talking while I excuse myself. Tell her we're thinking about one kid for now and get her going about the lake views."

"Okay," Kelsey managed to respond before Avery bounded back into the room. He'd need a helluva lot more caffeine to keep pace with her energy. Despite being used to waking up early—his alarm went off at four in the morning —and getting very little sleep during calving season—his max was three days—perky wasn't a word that would ever be used to describe his morning moods.

Hell, perky wouldn't be used anywhere near a description of him. The responsibility of caring for his brothers from a young age had made him grow up fast. He'd sat in for his parents at school meetings before he was old enough to shave. His mother's long trips to Houston left him in charge. His father was no better. The man left early in the morning and didn't return until past dark most nights, which left Kellan to make certain everyone got up, dressed, and out the door for school. Eight siblings. Most older kids who come from large families could probably attest to the fact you missed out on your own childhood.

Had Kellan built up a wall of resentment toward his parents?

Watching Aunt Lucia take care of the other side of the family might be responsible for some of the resentment he felt toward Adam, not to mention his own siblings. Holding onto those feelings wasn't productive.

"Here you go," Avery said, standing two feet from him, blinking at him while holding out her cell.

"If you'll excuse me," he said, taking the offering before heading out the back door onto the porch overlooking the lake. If he wasn't part of a family that owned more property than they could keep track of, this place would be a decent option. Could he buy a cabin and donate it?

Now that the Firebrands were getting along—on the surface anyway—the massive fortune his grandfather had built was shared equally. Basically giving Kellan more money than he knew what to do with.

The vehicle owner. He could donate the cabin to the owner of the vehicle he'd 'borrowed' not stolen. Borrowed was a better word. And true. He had every intention of bringing it back to its rightful owner. He could only hope that he hadn't caused too much distress to the owner in the meantime. The last thing someone needed after checking out of the hospital was to find their car had been 'taken' from the parking lot. Kellan couldn't bring himself to say the word *stolen* any longer.

Outside, he called family attorney Harlen Sawyer. The lawyer was a safe bet to pick up his cell and received multiple calls in a day, so it would be harder to track the call from Avery's phone back to Kellan. The attorney would also answer calls from unknown numbers when most ignored them.

Harlen picked up on the first ring. "Hello?"

"It's Kellan," he said. "And I don't have a lot of time to explain." He gave the elevator version of what had happened. Elevator version meaning if you only had an elevator ride to explain a situation, what would you say?

"How can I help?" Harlen asked.

"First of all, send someone to pick up a vehicle at..." Kellan glanced around, searching for a builder's sign. When he couldn't immediately find one, he settled on, "Lake Sticks at the new cabin development on the south end of the lake." He explained where the car could be found.

"Done," Harlen said, not wasting a second of time. "What next?"

"While the person you send is here, they need to stop into the model and ask for Avery," he continued. "I need them to buy one of the cabins with cash and gift it to the driver of the vehicle I borrowed from the hospital. Also, if there's a note on the car, pay it off."

"Done," Harlen said without hesitating. The Marshal had relied on his longtime friend and legal counsel since before Kellan was born. Harlen took his loyalty to the family seriously. "What else?"

"I need a vehicle, cash, and medical supplies to wrap an ankle stashed at the nearest gas station," he continued. "A change of clothes would be nice for me and a female, who is probably a small if I had to guess. And she needs shoes."

"Done."

Kellan rounded out the conversation asking for a grocery bag full of protein bars and fruit. "Sheriff Lawler needs to know that I'm safe, she's safe, and that I'll explain everything the minute I can."

"Okay-y-y-y." It was clear Harlen didn't like the sound of the last request.

"If I could tell you what that meant, I would," Kellan stated.

"I don't need to know," Harlen said. "Give me two hours for the rest."

"One more thing," Kellan said. "I need a burner phone."

"Got it."

Kellan turned around, saw Kelsey fidgeting out of the corner of his eye. Was she in trouble?

∼

Kelsey couldn't stall much longer.

"Should I grab the paperwork and get it started?" Avery pushed. The woman turned into a shark homing in on the vibration of a struggling fish.

"I-uh—"

Kellan walked in the back door before Kelsey was forced to answer.

"I have someone on the way to finalize the details of the

two-bedroom," he said. "Thank you for the use of your phone."

"My pleasure," Avery said, blinking at him. "Are you sure we haven't met?"

"Like I said, I fish around here so it's likely that's why I seem familiar," he said with a wink that caused Avery to blush. "This will be an amazing place to bring a little one." He walked straight to Kelsey and planted the kind of kiss that caused people to yell, "Get a room!"

It worked. Avery disappeared, probably leaving the 'couple' alone to celebrate.

Kelsey hadn't had much to celebrate when she'd been a couple. The idea of being a couple again might not be awful with Kellan but she couldn't see herself ever letting anyone else in. Trust was a slippery slope. She'd trusted all the promises Jackson had made years ago. Look where that had gotten her. A little voice in the back of her head pointed out that Kellan couldn't be further from Jackson.

Then there was the issue of building up a lie of a life. How would she ever return to Lone Star Pass again? The years of lying would mark her in a way that even a scarlet letter couldn't. The mark would be handed down to any children she might have.

Hold on.

When did she start thinking about children?

"Are you ready?" Kellan asked when he pulled back.

Her heart threatened to batter the inside of her ribs when his gaze caught hers. Her breath hitched. Her mouth dried up.

Instead of trying to summon her voice, she nodded.

Kellan held out an arm as Avery returned with a handful of paperwork.

"Let's just get a few details down before you skedaddle out of here," Avery practically chirped.

"We would stay if we could," Kellan countered as Kelsey pulled herself up by his arm. "I need to get her back to the campsite."

"Where are you?" Avery asked, ever persistent. "I can bring it to you or pick it up. Whatever works."

"What works is having my accountant bring a check and fill out the paperwork for me," Kellan said a little more sternly this time.

Avery blinked like someone had just thrown a punch. "Well, alright. I guess that'll work."

Did she fear her sale was slipping out the front door?

"Keep walking," Kellan said in barely above a whisper.

Kelsey gave a slight nod as her swollen ankle pounded her with pain, making it impossible to put any weight on it now.

Half-hopping, she managed to make it out the front door.

"Do you want me to drive you to your spot?" Avery called out in a last-ditch effort to keep them on the line.

"No. Thank you," Kellan responded, practically picking Kelsey up to get them out of there and away from Avery.

"I have a deeper understanding of what it means to be cornered by a pushy salesperson now," Kelsey said once they cleared the area.

Kellan picked her up and carried her honeymoon style deeper into the trees, artfully weaving in between branches. "She was determined."

"I know you're not a liar, Kellan. I'm sorry I made you one today."

"You didn't," he responded.

"Were you serious back there?" she asked. The shock in her voice amused him.

"The phone call I made was to my family's lawyer," he said. "We have about two hours to stay out of sight and get to the gas station nearest the entrance toward the cabin homes. But, yes, I asked him to send someone to buy one of the cabins and give it to the owner of the vehicle we borrowed last night as a thank you."

He set her down. "Hold on one sec. I need to return the fob."

True to his word, it didn't take long for Kellan to return and pick her up again. Kelsey would never understand having that kind of money. The kind that allowed someone to snap their fingers and buy a two-bedroom cabin. Her parents had barely scraped by. The congregation paid for the preacher's home and living expenses. The church was by no means wealthy but Kelsey had never wanted for anything as a child. She always had a roof over her head and food on the table. Her mother made a lot of Kelsey's clothes but the woman was an amazing seamstress. All Kelsey had to do was show her mother a picture and she could reproduce the outfit. Of course, her mother always made the skirt length a little longer than the model's but Kelsey couldn't complain.

Actually, she *had* complained as a teenager, but saw how silly she'd been now. It took hard times to ground a person, make them thankful for the smallest of things. Clean clothes ranked right up there along with having her laundry magically show up, folded on her bed. As a teen, she'd complained about walking into her room to find a stack of clothes on her bed.

How silly was that now?

As an adult who did her own laundry and a husband's

who couldn't seem to find the dirty clothes basket, let alone the laundry room in any of their many apartments.

Shame was funny. It kept her from coming home. It kept her from asking for help. It kept her from telling the truth about her situation.

Would her parents have been understanding?

Or would they have kept a strong line?

She would never know now that her father was gone and it was too late to talk to him. What she wouldn't give for one more conversation with her dad. Moisture gathered in her eyes.

"Where did you go just now?" Kellan broke through her heavy thoughts as he set her down on a log. He took the spot right next to her, sitting shoulder-to-shoulder. Well, it would be shoulder-to-shoulder if he wasn't so tall. It was more like arm-to-her shoulder.

"Sorry," she said, shaking her head to shake off some of the heaviness that came with thinking about her father. "That was really nice of you to do, by the way." She didn't want to go into it with Kellan about what she'd been thinking.

"I didn't ask for the money," he said, surprising her.

"Why not?" she asked. "I mean, from my point of view, it sure would have made my life easier."

"That's understandable," he agreed. "I'm not saying it's a curse. But it's a strange feeling to have a boatload of money dropped in your lap when you didn't do anything to earn it."

"You've lived your whole life on that ranch, working," she pointed out. "If you ask me, its success is exactly linked to you and the others. You should all share in the benefits."

"Maybe," he tentatively agreed. "I just don't want it to change me."

After hearing about his mother, she completely understood how deep that comment must run.

"It won't. It couldn't." Kelsey wrapped her arm around his and leaned into him. "Because you're a good person, Kellan."

"That's debatable," he quipped. "And it depends on who you ask. For instance, I doubt my ex would agree with that statement. Or my cousin Corbin, who is now her husband."

"You are," she insisted. "Who else would help someone like me? Still give me compliments even after you've heard my story and about all my mistakes? And then cover my tracks after putting you in a position to make you lie and steal?"

"Best adventure I've been on in one helluva long time," he said with a chuckle.

She could only hope it wouldn't end up killing him.

10

Kellan wasn't letting Kelsey get away with calling him a saint. "I've been a jerk to people who were trying to help me. I was a huge asshole to my ex-wife. I'm certain there's a long list of people who would contest my nomination into sainthood because I'm doing the right thing and helping you."

"I doubt it," Kelsey said without hesitation. He liked seeing himself through her eyes. "And, besides, even if you've made mistakes." She flashed eyes at him. "Like you'd have me to believe everyone does. People can change."

"True," he agreed. "It's never too late."

"No," she said. "It isn't."

She seemed unaware of the path he was walking her down. Then again, Kelsey was savvy. The likelihood she'd figured him out was high.

"Have you thought about visiting your mom while you're here?" he asked.

"Only about a hundred times," she said on a sharp sigh. "But I have no intention of dragging my problems to her front door. The less she knows about my current situation, the safer she'll be. Plus, someone could be watching her house."

"Once the bastard who is following you is arrested, you won't have to worry about any of that," he said.

"If," she corrected.

Since arguing would do no good, he let it go. He would find the person responsible for her current situation and take the asshole down himself.

"Either way, it's good to see you again, Kellan."

"Same here," he said. A little too good?

Probably.

Kelsey's life wasn't in Lone Star Pass anymore and he had no plans to leave the ranch. It was where he belonged, even if it didn't quite feel like home. Strangely enough, Kelsey did, which was odd at best.

Was it their shared history? However brief those moments between them, all those years ago, had been? The current situation? Bonding out of trauma?

Kellan wasn't the type to look backward. It never did any good as far as he was concerned. The past couldn't be changed. A few things bugged him, though. The divorce. He hadn't handled it well. The fact that Adam had moved into the Marshal's home. The fact he'd let Kelsey slip out of his fingers.

"If I'd asked you out back in high school, would you have said yes?" he asked. Why not?

"Does it really matter now?" came the response. He hadn't been expecting a question in answer to his question.

Those words were going to leave fresh scars. If it didn't matter to him, he wouldn't have asked. Before he could continue down that road, she scooted away from him.

"What's next, Kellan? Where do we go? What do we do?" she asked, clearly uncomfortable with having that conversation. They might not be able to change the past but he wanted to know.

He noted that she'd changed the topic. This wasn't the time to press the issue.

"You can't keep running forever," he pointed out, circling back to the current problem.

"I'd like to catch my breath for once," she said on a sharp exhale. "It feels like I'm always running from something. Hiding."

"Real sleep would be good at this point," he added. "And a decent meal." Could he take her back to the ranch?

No. Now that he'd stolen a vehicle, it might not be safe for him to go back to the ranch either.

Maybe it was better to put one foot in front of the other. They had two hours to kill before help would arrive at the gas station. Being back in the cold caused Kelsey to shiver. He wrapped an arm around her, pulling her closer under the guise of body heat. The sweater she'd found wasn't enough to keep her warm. She leaned into him again, a perfect fit.

"Where is this magical place we can get good sleep?" she asked. "Because that sounds like heaven right now."

"I'm working on it," he reassured. There were pay-by-the-hour motels along the highway. He could get a room with a bed, a shower, and a coffee maker. As much as he disliked the idea of one of those places, he was short on quality options. Calling anyone else would only put the person in danger or risk of arrest. The call to Sawyer had been risky enough.

"It doesn't have to be fancy, if that's worrying you," she

said. "I've lived in some pretty awful places and survived. Another night wouldn't hurt anything. Plus, it would give us a chance to think clearly once we get some rest and shift out of emergency mode."

Kellan thought about the way he left the hospital, what the sheriff must be thinking, and how awful it must have been for the vehicle owner to walk outside and realize their transportation had been taken from them. He could only hope his gestures were enough of an apology.

Kellan wanted to do right by people. It wouldn't be fair of him to expect Adam to think about those things if Kellan didn't walk the talk. He could see that clearly now.

The Marshal had all but ruined one generation of Firebrand men. Kellan wasn't letting his grandfather take the second generation as well. Which meant change on his part too. He was beginning to see that now.

"How long has it been since we left the cabin?" Kelsey asked.

"Forty-five minutes," he said. "A vehicle with supplies will be waiting on us in another hour and fifteen minutes. It'll probably take us forty-five minutes to walk to the gas station from here but that's just a guess on my part."

"How long would it take you if I wasn't in the picture?" she asked.

"I'd be able to make the run in half that time, maybe less," he admitted, unsure where this was going, but not liking where it seemed to be headed.

"You should go without me," she said firmly.

"I'm not leaving you here alone." Period. Kellan had no plans to leave her to fend for herself in her current vulnerable state.

"It makes sense to do it that way," she argued.

"Not in my book."

"Kellan, think about it. Please. You won't have to leave as soon." Kelsey used those incredible violet eyes to try and persuade him. It wasn't going to work.

"What happens if this guy catches up to you while I'm not here?" he asked.

"I'll hide," she offered. "We can find a good spot for me where he won't find me."

Kellan shook his head. "I don't like it."

"But you can admit that it makes more sense to do it that way, right?" She glanced down at her swollen ankle.

"Logically, you'll get no argument from me," he said. "There's more to it than that."

"Then explain because I'm not seeing how it'll hurt anything," she said. "I can't put any more pressure on this ankle. We'll be noticed together with you helping me walk. Won't that make us stand out even more?"

"Maybe."

"Then, why not leave me here so you can get the vehicle and get back faster?" she asked, her face twisted in confusion.

"Because I can't do that," he said.

"What does that mean?" she asked. "You can't? Or won't?"

"There a difference?" he questioned.

"Fair point," she conceded.

"We'll leave in half an hour," he said. "That'll give you plenty of time to rest that ankle." He studied it, not liking how swollen it was.

"Even with your help, walking is hard, Kellan. I can't put any weight on this foot. I'm tired. I'll only slow you down."

"If I have to carry you the whole way, I will," he stated.

"Why?" she asked.

"Because you disappeared on me once and I'm not letting it happen again," he said with a little more anger than intended.

∽

"I'm not going anywhere," Kelsey said, trying to hide the sting that came with his words. For a split-second, she wondered if he was talking about the hospital or high school.

The hospital, she decided. High school was a long time ago.

After opening up and talking about the past, Kelsey had hoped to gain Kellan's trust. As it was, she had a long way to go.

He was right about one thing, though. She would disappear from his life if she had another option. He didn't deserve to have his world turned upside down because of her. He'd been right about another thing too. She couldn't run forever. It was only a matter of time before the bastard who was after her caught up again. Then what?

Going back to her vehicle was out of the question now that word was out that she was in town. She'd given her statement to the sheriff, who would have sent a deputy to investigate by now. Crime scene tape would be used to cordon off the area where she'd been run off the road. All her belongings would be removed—if they hadn't been already—and logged as evidence. There was no way she could get those back without a trip to the sheriff's office. Even then, she was far more likely to end up arrested for grand theft auto. That had to be a felony.

Damn. It occurred to her the hospital staff would talk about her being home. She would most likely be a hot topic of conversation, especially coming in injured and with a Firebrand. Word would get back to her mother, as if she deserved more pain caused by her only child. The lies Kelsey had carefully constructed to protect her mother were about to come crashing around her.

Surprisingly, she felt a sense of relief when she'd convinced herself the truth coming out would be so much worse. All the hiding, all the deception had been like having a chain around her that was connected to a cement block.

The truth, it turned out, was liberating.

Except as rumors ran rampant around town that Kelsey was seen, her mother would be in more danger. So, she needed to circle back to Dallas and stand her ground for better or worse. This had to stop.

And then if she survived, her next stop would be to her mother's house where she would tell her everything.

More of those chains broke off at the thought. Sadness for the life she'd been living replaced the momentary relief. Too much time had been wasted. Too much of her life had been spent worrying about what other people would think of her if she got a divorce. Guess what? She was divorced anyway, despite her best efforts to stay married. Jackson hadn't wanted to be in the marriage any more than she had. Had he stuck around as long as he did because he felt responsible for her in some way? Because she walked away from her parents to be with him?

"I know where we need to go," she said to Kellan.

He studied her for a long moment before saying, "Dallas."

"That's right," she said. "You made a good point earlier when you said we should be going after the source. Whoever ran me off the road is nothing more than an errand boy." That also meant going back to her former place of employment. Kelsey involuntarily shivered at the thought of going back to the bar. Removing herself from it had been the second-best thing about her current circumstances.

Kellan sat there for a long moment.

"I'm not going to disappear again, Kellan."

He didn't respond.

"You can trust me," she added. "I give my word."

After a few moments passed, he gave a slight nod.

"We pick up the vehicle," she continued, not looking a gift horse in the mouth. "And then make the drive to Dallas. Everyone believes we're here in Lone Star Pass, so the trip to Dallas will be unexpected."

"There's a problem," he countered. "We're wanted by the law."

"We can't be certain of that," she said.

"Our fingerprints will be all over the stolen vehicle," he said. "Avery will be able to confirm we were at the lake. She will tell them everything, not to mention the sale."

"That's not a crime," she said. "And doesn't the person who owned the car have to file a complaint?"

"What are you getting at?" he asked.

"I'm just saying the car was borrowed," she stated. "We gave it back, or, at least, will give it back soon."

"No harm, no foul?"

"Exactly," she agreed.

"The car's owner might not see it the same way despite getting a free property out of it," he pointed out.

"We'll cross that bridge when we come to it, but my guess is that they'll be fine," she said. "I'm not pretending to have all the answers. But for the first time since we left the hospital parking lot, I have hope. I'm unwilling to give it up easily."

"Okay," he said. "Say we get to Dallas without being stopped or found by the bastard who has been chasing you."

"It's possible," she said, hearing the optimism in her own voice. "The next part is trickier, for sure. Maybe we stop off and find a motel. Get a few hours of sleep and take a little more time figuring out the next step. All I know is if I show my face at the club, the guys searching for me will get word."

His eyebrow arched. "And you were thinking that was a good idea?"

"It is if we want to flesh them out of the dark corners where they are currently hiding," she said.

"I'll do my best to get us to Dallas without ending up behind bars or six feet under," he said. "Did you check the cargo you were carrying for them on this errand you're supposed to be running?"

"Yes," she said. "It was a box of weapons."

"Why would you need to deliver a few guns?" he asked.

"I had the same question but I also realized it wasn't my business to ask," she said.

"Weapons runners would normally have more cargo than a box," he said. "How big is the box?"

"Trunk-sized. About the size of a box you'd use to pack clothes in if you were moving," she said. "I thought it was strange at the time too."

"Where is that box now?"

"You asked me that question before," she said. "Telling you digs a deeper hole for you, Kellan. Are you sure you want that?"

"How much deeper can I get without actually being you?" he quipped. He had a point. "I already told you that I'm going the distance with you on this. I'm just as wanted for questioning as you are at this point. I'm not leaving you alone to deal with this on your own."

"There'll be no turning back if I tell you where the evidence is," she warned.

"I know."

Kelsey gave him the location of the storage unit down to the unit's number. And then it dawned on her why the box was so small and needed to be buried. *Evidence.*

11

"The box isn't filled with guns for sale. It's filled with evidence," Kelsey said at the same time Kellan thought it.

"My mind just went there too," he confided. "The contents of that box might link murderers to their crimes."

"Wouldn't they have enough sense to wipe them down?" she asked.

"Yes," Kellan agreed. "However, cases can be thrown out if there's no murder weapon. A good lawyer can have a field day with that in court, if a case made it that far without one. Plus casings can be matched to guns."

"Those are good points," she said, her violet eyes lighting up with more hope. "We might be able to put very bad people away for a long time with that box." She bit down on her bottom lip. "Maybe have a chance to make up for my past wrongs in the process."

If anyone was in need of redemption, it was him. As far as he was concerned, Kelsey had learned to survive in awful conditions. She'd made mistakes, like everyone did, when she was young and had been living the consequences of them far too long.

Everyone was entitled to mess up every once in a while. No one was perfect. Would she be able to see that once this was behind her?

Kellan checked the time. "We should get going."

"Okay," she said, shifting her gaze to her ankle. "I still think it would be better for you to go. You'll be less conspicuous if you really think about it. Even if folks are looking for the 'thieves' they'll be searching for a couple. I'm injured so that would be part of the news too. The gossip hounds have had time to spread the latest about me. It'll be news. My fall from grace at the time of my father's death. The hounds will come out and damage his reputation as a preacher." She blew out a breath. "Say what you want about his parenting skills, but my father cared about his calling. He cared about the congregation. He cared about everyone but me, turns out."

Kellan held her tight against him for a long moment. As much as he didn't want to admit it, carrying her for forty-five minutes would be next to impossible given his current energy level. Forcing her to move would only make that ankle worse. There would be supplies inside the vehicle to wrap it. "Tell you what. You stay here. I'll grab the vehicle and come right back."

"Okay," she said, then sucked in a breath. "What if you get caught?"

"No matter how we play this, there are risks," he pointed out. Her nerves were getting the best of her. She'd made excellent arguments for staying put before. "It'll be okay, Kelsey." He could reassure her, but not make a promise he couldn't keep.

"I know," she said before her mouth found his.

The kiss, which wasn't more than lips grazing, had more erotic promise than anything Kellan had experienced before. He'd never had this same level of heat with Liv, despite being married to her for a short time and being in love at the time. Their relationship had been one-sided. Was that the reason?

"Stay right here unless you hear something," he warned. "Then, you know what to do."

"What if it's you, coming back to me?" she asked.

"I'll whistle like this," he said, mimicking bird sounds.

"Got it," she said before bringing her hand up to his face. "Come back to me in one piece. Okay?"

He nodded, pressed a quick kiss to her lips, then took off in the direction of the highway. Years of fishing in the area gave him the lay of the land even though it had been a while since he'd come to this spot. The development might be new but the rest was coming back to him as he jogged through the dense trees and tried not to get tangled in scrub brush.

The logistics of getting to the vehicle and back should be easy enough without interference. Jogging wasn't a problem now that his lungs had had time to clear. Thankfully, the smoke didn't appear to have caused serious damage.

Jogging to the gas station took a little less than twenty minutes. The Chevron was on the opposite side of the highway, so he'd had to play a game of human Frogger to get across since there was no underpass within running distance.

The place was hopping. There were four vehicles parked off to one side with no one nearby. Several of the pumps were full. And half a dozen was parked in the spaces directly in front of the building. His vehicle would be one of the four. He had no idea what he was looking for. People walked in and out of the convenience store.

He'd have to check out the four vehicles to the right and hope he didn't draw any attention while he figured out which one was his. The thought occurred to him that Sawyer might not have had enough time to gather everything and get a vehicle out here. This would be the first time Kellan would be accused of being too early for anything. Hell, most of the time he joked he'd be late to his own funeral.

At this point, he hoped that day wasn't in his near future. Kelsey being in possession of weapons that could lock several bad guys away for a very long time wasn't helping with her longevity. Folks like that—if they were right about the origin of the weapons—would have nothing to lose. They would think nothing of wiping Kellan and Kelsey off the face of the earth.

Did they suspect she'd already gone to the law?

Would the driver in the hoodie have run her off the road if they did? He doubted it, but these were all just guesses at this point. He cut across the lot, looking like he had a purpose. It was surprising how many folks left him alone if he kept his head down and walked with purpose. Even in a town like Lone Star Pass, where folks prided themselves on saying hello to their neighbors. The town had its friendly side, especially if you weren't from the wrong side of the Firebrand family tree.

Of course, those same folks smiled to your face. Apparently, the knife twisted better if you didn't see it coming.

Kellan could admit he hadn't made much effort in changing anyone's opinion. His temper didn't help matters. He knew better than to let it take the wheel. He was getting too old for excuses.

Time to cowboy up. Or, in his case, rancher up. Face the music. Move on.

A new kind of life was in his sights now. A family of his own, which wasn't something he ever believed he would want after the divorce.

Damn. He owed Liv an apology. Corbin too.

The vehicles were two sedans, a truck, and an SUV complete with a soccer mom sticker on the back. He ruled the last one out almost immediately. Sawyer wouldn't do that to him, would he?

As he approached the first sedan, a man stepped out of the store and made a beeline toward Kellan. He dropped down and pretended to tie his shoelaces a little too late because he had on boots.

Cool. Good one, Kellan.

Whistling usually caused folks to glance at him and then look away. It worked this time too.

The man went to the first sedan. That was a close one.

Kellan hesitated, giving the man plenty of time to back out of the spot and then exit the parking lot. Being close to the highway meant most of the drivers were in a hurry. This wasn't the Piggly Wiggly where folks stopped in the parking lot to chat for half an hour before buying groceries. Highway gas stations were usually filled with folks who had somewhere to be and wanted to get back on the highway to get there.

One sedan was left, the truck, and the dreaded SUV.

Taking in a deep breath, Kellan went for the truck. The doors were locked. Before an alarm blared, he took a step back. Sawyer would leave instructions not to lock the vehicle. Unless, of course, the key was on top of the back tire. Would Sawyer think to give that instruction?

This time, Kellan tried the passenger side of the sedan. No dice. It was locked as well.

That left the SUV. He prayed the doors would be locked. Although, to be honest, he wasn't in a position to be too picky. Plus, Sawyer had had to scramble to get the vehicle here. Kellan was in no position to look down on the ride provided for him, considering he was a fugitive.

Possibly a fugitive.

Kellan sidled up to the handle of the SUV. In one motion, he grabbed it. Locked.

Either the vehicle wasn't here yet, or the key was sitting on the back tire. Waiting. Hanging around the vehicles, trying each one would draw attention if he didn't figure it out soon. Once again, he acted as if he was supposed to be here, and moved with purpose. A quick skim to get the lay of the land revealed no one seemed too interested in his activities yet.

Turning his back to the store was a risky move, but he had to in order to check for keys. *Please be the truck.*

Kellan liked trucks. Trucks blended in. A sedan would do okay too. They would be a little more exposed in a smaller vehicle but he could make it work.

As he reached for the back tire on the driver's side of the truck, he glanced around and saw an angry-faced cowboy staring him down as he walked directly toward Kellan. He withdrew his hand and dropped onto all fours.

"Can I help you with something?" the cowboy asked, his voice full of piss and vinegar. Was he looking for a fight?

"Dropped my key," Kellan mumbled, fake feeling around underneath the truck. "Here you are."

The cowboy stopped a few feet back. From the corner of Kellan's eye, he saw the tall, thin guy fold his arms over his chest.

Kellan made a show of pocketing the non-existent key, keeping his fist closed to hide the fact there was none. He hopped to standing and then nodded as he walked past the cowboy, who sized him up for a second and then seemed to think better of starting anything.

He turned toward the store, figuring the cowboy would get inside the truck and pull out before he made it halfway across the lot.

The cowboy didn't.

In fact, he sat in his vehicle staring at his phone.

Dammit.

Kellan didn't want to go inside and risk anyone recognizing him. Being a Firebrand had that effect even out here by Lake Stick. Worrying about Kelsey distracted him. Leaving her alone in the woods wasn't exactly his idea of warm and fuzzy.

Instead of walking into the front door, he kept going and circled the building.

Cowboy was still sitting there.

∼

KELSEY PALMED the sharp rock she'd found on the ground next to the log, shivering in the cold morning air. At least the sun was up, warming her enough to stop her teeth from chattering. The woods were coming alive too. Every sound tightened the tension in her neck and shoulders. She rolled them a few times in a vain attempt to release some of the knots. At this point, her muscles were the equivalent of a traffic pile-up on an icy highway.

The sound of twigs crunching to her left sent her pulse racing. Maybe Kellan was right. Maybe it was a bad idea to leave her here alone.

Moving would alert the twig-snapper to her location next to the tree trunk, so she leaned against the base of the tree, and hoped whatever made the noise moved on. Preferably in the opposite direction.

There were plenty of possibilities aside from the obvious one. Deer were plentiful out here. Her mind snapped to illegal hunting. A person with a gun wasn't someone she cared to run into in her present condition.

There would be questions.

Should she think up a backstory?

Kelsey shook her head. She didn't have any more lies or deceptions in her. Telling Kellan the truth about her past, her life, had given her a sense of lightness she had almost forgotten existed. So, no more lies. No more half-truths.

Didn't mean she had to unload her whole life story on a stranger but she could honestly say that her ankle was injured and she was waiting on her friend to go get a car. If she was lucky, the person—if that was in fact what she was dealing with—wouldn't recognize her or ask follow-up questions.

The twig-breaker must have bolted based on the sounds now. An animal?

Kelsey exhaled. And then she sat there, looking through the barren trees to the water beyond. It was only a glimpse but there was something calming about being near water, watching the sparkles as the sun kissed the small waves. She could sit here for days.

Hand-in-hand, her father used to take her for long walks when she was a little girl. She'd looked up to him like he was a saint. Finding out he wasn't the person she'd believed he was in later years had knocked the wind out of her.

Tears spilled out of her eyes. She remembered. It was a memory she'd tucked down so deep that even she couldn't access it. She'd been seventeen years old when she'd seen her father with the church accountant behind closed doors. The two of them locked in a passionate kiss—the kind that had real heat, unlike the pecks on the cheek he gave Kelsey's mother.

Kelsey had blocked out the memory because she would never hurt her mother like that. But a wall came up between her and her parents that day. Crushing her mother by telling her that her husband was having an affair wasn't something Kelsey could do. She loved her mother. She wondered if her mother suspected. She'd spent sleepless nights for weeks trying to decide the right thing to do.

In the end, she'd kept her father's dirty secret. And he never knew she'd been the wiser.

More tears fell.

The way he'd looked at her, judged her, when she said she was in love and wanted to get married still hurt.

"Marrying too young is a mistake you'll regret for the rest of your life," he'd said. He'd married Kelsey's mother when they were both nineteen.

Had he been trapped in a loveless marriage?

Didn't matter. Her mother deserved better.

Salty tears streamed down her face now. She sniffled and coughed, trying to find a way to stem the flow but it was no use. The floodgates were open.

Would Kelsey have been better off not knowing Jackson cheated on their marriage? It might have been kinder for him to just leave with no explanation. Their marriage had been dead for so long anyway. It wasn't like the news would have come as a shock. In some ways, she might have even been waiting for it.

But, no, she'd left well enough alone.

Kelsey's mother had a cheating husband who the town thought was some kind of saint, not to mention a divorced daughter.

"Are you alright?" a familiar male voice asked. Panic gripped her. She remembered the voice from last night.

12

By the time Kellan circled the building a second time, another vehicle drove up and parked next to the remaining sedan and SUV. He leaned against the side of the building, pretending to hold a phone. From a distance, it might not be obvious he stared at his flat palm.

The driver exited the Jeep and then headed into the store.

Kellan quickly moved into action. With the way his luck was going, the SUV was going to be his, so he stopped there first. The key fob sat on the back tire. At least the SUV's windows were blacked out and it was large enough for the two of them to sleep inside if push came to shove and they had to pull over and rest.

In fact, a rest stop wasn't such a bad idea.

Inside the gold-colored SUV, he saw a cooler in the backseat and two bags filled with clothes. In the console, he located a cell phone, a burner that would be next to impossible to trace back to him.

The engine started with a button push. Kellan put the gearshift in reverse and then pulled out of the parking spot.

He'd been away from Kelsey too long. With every passing minute, his stress levels jumped up another notch, heading toward panic at a break-neck pace by this point.

The thought of her being in the woods, alone, vulnerable caused his chest to squeeze. Losing her when he'd just gotten her back wasn't something he could consider. If she was caught, she would end up in jail. He wasn't certain if the law would go easy on her after they'd stolen a car. Knowing her, she would take full responsibility in order to protect him. Then what?

She could reveal the location of the weapons but what if they couldn't be tied to a specific crime? Or a certain criminal?

Fingerprints would have been removed. Surely, killers would be smart enough to erase evidence directly linking them to their crimes.

Kelsey had mentioned she had no idea why she'd been chosen for the 'errand' as it had been called. Figure that out, and they could get to the bottom of who was trying to erase her now.

Kellan made a U-turn half a mile down the road before hightailing it to the next right on his way to Kelsey. A bad feeling took hold in the pit of his stomach.

Speeding would be one sure way to draw attention and possibly end up pulled over, so he'd kept it cool. A soccer mom vehicle wouldn't stick out here. Sawyer's move was genius even though this was the last vehicle Kellan wanted to drive. He could have switched plates on the 'borrowed' car with Avery's once she came into work and gotten farther down the road. He would have had to switch plates several times before making it to Dallas. Each time he stopped would invite unwanted risk.

But it would have been an option.

Parking closest to the spot where he'd left Kelsey, he hopped out of the vehicle, locked the doors, and made a beeline toward the log. As he neared, he heard voices. Kelsey was talking to someone. Who?

Pulling on all his years of experience tracking poachers, he moved without making a sound through the trees. He made a wide turn to come at them from the opposite angle. The minute Kelsey came into view, his heart skipped a beat. Because sitting beside her on the log was the old man from last night.

No shotgun this time, so that was probably a good sign.

The last thing Kellan expected happened. The two hugged. Then, the older gentleman stood up and turned back the way he came toward his home. Kellan assumed the man had been out for a morning walk before happening upon Kelsey. What story did she make up to get the man moving?

When the coast was clear, Kellan joined her.

"What was that all about?" he asked, noticing her tear-stained cheeks as he approached.

"Mr. Wisel," she said before wiping tears from her face. "He found me and asked if he could sit with me for a while."

Kellan moved next to her and sat down. She scooted closer to him and wrapped her arm around his. Having her this close both calmed and excited him at the same time. An interesting mix.

"I wasn't sure how to respond," she admitted. "But then I said yes." She paused. "He asked me why I was crying." She turned those violet eyes on Kellan, causing his chest to squeeze. "With everything that has happened, I realized how much I wish I could have said goodbye to my dad before he died. Now, there's no chance to apologize or tell him how my life turned out. He would have been disappointed but at least I would have been honest with him. The fact he lied to my mother about an affair made me resent him so much that I think I ended up punishing myself more."

"Families are complicated," Kellan agreed. He needed to make peace while everyone was still alive and willing, including his mother. "There's no handbook on how to deal with them. We do the best we can and hope it's enough."

"That's true," she agreed. "I just don't want to have any more regrets, which is why I'm going to tell my mother everything if I make it out of here alive."

"We will," he reassured, more determined than ever.

The cell he'd pocketed vibrated in his pocket. This was the worst possible time to check it, except that only one person had this number.

He shot a look of apology at Kelsey and fished the cell out of his pocket. The text from Sawyer read:

It's your uncle. He's had another stroke.

The text was followed by the words no one wants to hear with news like that:

I'm sorry for your loss.

"What is it, Kellan?" Kelsey asked, leaning in to read the screen. He tilted it toward her.

She brought her hand up to her mouth to cover a gasp. "I'm so sorry. You shouldn't be here with me. Go to your family, Kellan."

How did he tell her that she was his family too?

Simple. He didn't.

"Once this is over, I'll go," he said. "But I'm not leaving you."

Kellan responded:

Pls send my love to the family. I'll be home soon.

"If you hadn't gotten mixed up with me, you would be with them," she said so low that he almost didn't hear her.

"I'm right where I'm supposed to be, Kelsey," he said. "My family is big. They have each other. Who do you have?"

Kelsey stared out ahead of them at the water.

"Don't push me away," he said. "Me being at home won't change a thing. Besides, the service won't be held right away. I won't miss that."

"You can't be certain of that, Kellan. Not as long as you're with me," she said.

"Let me help you, Kelsey."

Would she?

᠅

As much as Kelsey wanted Kellan right by her side, his family came first. The thought of being away from him again sent waves of panic rushing through her, but he'd just lost his uncle and he needed to go home.

"We can't stay here much longer," Kellan said. "We need to get on the road now that I have a vehicle. Someone will be picking up the sedan we borrowed, and news will get out that we were here. Avery might have connected the dots by now. She might have discovered the vehicle after we left. She might have called the law. They could be one step behind us. All we know for certain is that we have to leave."

"You're right," she agreed. "But I wish there was some way you could go home first." As much as it pained her to take him away from his family right now, she wouldn't argue. She wouldn't make it a mile without him. For the first time in longer than she could remember, she could depend on someone else.

Selfish as it might be, she didn't want the feeling to end.

"That's the first place Sheriff Lawler would look," he pointed out.

"Okay," she said because he was right and that would lead to consequences they weren't ready to face. "But we end this soon and get you back to Lone Star Pass to be with your family."

Kellan stood up and picked her up without another word, which surprised her. Maybe he wasn't looking a gift horse in the mouth because she didn't put up an argument about leaving. Maybe he knew better than to linger or she might change her mind and try to convince him to stay.

If anything bad happened to him because of her, she could never forgive herself.

Kellan booked it to the waiting vehicle, an SUV. It was big and shouldn't draw attention, especially in Dallas where it seemed every soccer mom drove one at a hundred miles an hour with kids in the back.

The thought of going back to the club after coming home sent a swirl of dread spiraling through her, landing hard in the pit of her stomach. Her past self was about to crash into her present.

Not anymore. No. She'd left the business. She was never going back. Even if she had to spend her nights sleeping in a tent, she would find another way to make money.

Because strangely enough the life she left was worth fighting to get back to.

∽

BEING BACK on the North Dallas Tollway, or NDT as everyone called it now, caused a well of memories to spring up. Facing them head-on instead of running away was the only way to put this chapter behind Kelsey.

Life might have dealt a few blows, but she'd also learned how to survive on her own. She'd learned to stand on her own two feet with no education past high school and no preparation for the real world.

A renewed sense of pride filled her. Had she made mistakes? The short answer was yes. Had her life been perfect? Far from it. But she'd learned to depend on herself. She'd kept food on the table. Jackson certainly hadn't. He'd been too invested in his music career and she'd been too eager to play a supporting role in his life.

When and if—and it was a big *if*—she ever decided to let another person in her life, she would play a starring role. She would find a partner, an equal, instead of someone who didn't see her worth.

If you don't see your worth, no one else will. The one voice from the back of her mind she could trust had made this a mantra. Now? She knew it to be true.

Kelsey stared out the window as they passed her former place of employment. Even the building of Naked, Not Afraid looked dirtier in the daylight as they drove past. It was early evening at this point, before sunset. They'd stopped off at a rest stop on the way to Dallas to grab a couple hours of sleep. The spot off the highway had showers. Clean clothes had miraculously shown up with the SUV, along with a few other necessities, including a pair of shoes.

"Where to?" Kellan asked. He was a fish out of water in a big city.

"There's a rent-by-the-night motel nearby," she said. "We could regroup there, use it as a home base."

"Okay," he agreed. Everything was easy with Kellan. With Jackson, if she said *red*, he said *blue*. At one point, she was convinced that he did it just to make things difficult for her.

Neither she nor Kellan had said much on the ride to Dallas. Being quiet with Kellan was her new favorite thing. It was peace like she'd never known.

Actually, that wasn't true. She'd felt the same thing back in high school that special night with him. And then missed it for a lifetime.

Back then, and for years after, she'd convinced herself the intense feeling was teenage hormones and nothing more. She'd managed to believe that she loved Jackson after dating for a while too. Her feelings toward her ex, she'd learned, put her in a caregiver role.

Kelsey knew the difference now. The feelings she'd felt for Kellan were the real deal. She'd been vulnerable with him in a way she'd never been with Jackson.

Now? She would settle for nothing less if she could ever let herself go down that road again with anyone.

Turning to get one more look at Naked, Not Afraid, she caught sight of something that stopped her cold.

"What's Jackson's car doing parked at the club?" she asked, craning her neck to make sure. Had he found her?

"Did he know you worked there?" Kellan asked.

"I never told a soul," she admitted. "I was far too embarrassed to say I worked at a strip club."

"What about your neighbors?" he asked.

"No one," she said. Why on earth would her ex show up at the club?

"Is your divorce final?" he asked.

"It is now," she said. "We couldn't afford to file right away. I couldn't, at least. Divorce costs money that I didn't have." Maybe that was it. Jackson had a change of heart? Was he trying to reverse the divorce? It was too late for that, but he might not realize it. She couldn't for the life of her figure out why Jackson would come back. And then it dawned on her. "Actually, never mind. He must be sniffing around for money. He must think I have some now since I didn't go running back to Lone Star Pass. He must think that I have a stash of cash somewhere."

The man was batshit ridiculous if he thought she would entertain the idea of being a couple again.

"Or he might have realized that he made the biggest mistake of his life when he walked out on you and has come back to beg forgiveness," Kellan said, a hint of jealousy in his tone.

Did he believe she would take Jackson back? Because it hurt like hell that he would be convinced of such a thing. Her heart knew what it wanted. Did Kellan not realize it was him?

13

"If Jackson thinks I want to be in the same room with him again, the man has another think coming," Kelsey said.

Was it that easy? Kellan had lost out to the man once.

Hold on there, Firebrand. You have no designs on Kelsey. You didn't years ago as much as you might have wanted to and you don't now.

"After what he put me through, the man doesn't need to darken my doorway again. Ever. But if he does, you know what? I'm so over the whole situation that I might just laugh."

Walking away from Liv had been hard. Kellan had held onto resentment for the divorce. Would he go back even if that was an option?

Hell, no.

Life moved on. Liv and Corbin should have been together from the get-go. Kellan could see that now. Life had a way of working out the kinks. His foolish heart had survived. But in those early days, he would have taken her back to stop the ache in his chest.

Would Kelsey?

"By the time we come back tonight, he might be gone," Kellan said. He almost wished they would run into the man. Kellan would be able to tell by Kelsey's reaction if she still had feelings for her ex.

"Good," she said before pinching the bridge of her nose as though stemming a headache. "But you know what? It doesn't really matter to me anymore. There was a time when I was so hurt that I wanted to lash out at him. Let him see how much he hurt me. But then I realized the man doesn't deserve my energy, my time, or my breath. I embraced the best three words when it came to my relationship with him, *Let it go*. And everything shifted after that. Would I appreciate it if Jackson came back to pay back the money he took from me? I'm not going to lie, the answer to that question is a resounding yes. But, I've been surviving and a whole lot happier without him." She put her hands up, palms out, in the surrender position. "I'm still working my way out of debt and will be for a long time but I see that it's possible. I just have to stay the course. I've been realizing that too late, though. I shouldn't have tried to take a shortcut, Kellan."

He liked the way his name rolled off her tongue so easily.

"People make mistakes, Kelsey," he pointed out. "Last time I checked, you're 'people.'"

"Some of them have consequences that are more than we bargained for," she said.

"Have you thought about taking the weapons to Sheriff Lawler?" he asked. "He's clean. You can trust him."

"What if they came after my mom?" she asked. "The scandal, the gossip alone would be worse than awful after losing my dad but these awful men might hurt her to get back at me."

Kellan saw a sign for a motel. "Is this the place you were talking about?"

"Yes," she said with an involuntary shiver. "I know. It's beyond gross. We just won't sit on anything."

"I might have a better idea," he said, thinking there had to be a place that would be discreet in Dallas, where stars and star athletes came on a regular basis. He pulled off to the side of the road and called Harlen.

The attorney picked up on the first ring.

"I'm sorry about your uncle, Kellan," Sawyer said, "but I have more news. Are you driving?"

"No." Kellan didn't like the sound of that. "Why? What is it?"

"Sitting down?"

"I'm good," Kellan reassured. "What happened now?"

"Upon hearing the news of your uncle's passing, your father had a catastrophic heart attack," Sawyer said. "My phone was in my hand just now because I was about to call you with the news your father didn't make it."

Kellan wasn't sure what to say next. Shock robbed his voice but no words came anyway. His first thought was how awful this would be for his mother and the sadness that came with knowing he wouldn't get to see his father one last time. His mother, however, had lost her freedom and now her husband. It was a lot for anyone to handle. Would the news drag her under again? "Has anyone contacted my mother?"

"She was the first to be notified, since she was next of kind," Harlen said, his voice full of compassion. "In fact, she called me."

"How did she sound?" he asked, figuring this could break her. The abuse she'd suffered at the hands of her uncle as a little girl, paired with the fact her parents didn't believe her when she plucked up the courage to speak up about it, had broken her. What would this do? Would she stop fighting? Would she harm herself?

"Stronger than you might think," Harlen stated, surprising him. "She mentioned wanting to be strong for her sons, who she said would need her more than ever now."

Relief washed over him. He could only hope her resolve would last. "That's good to hear. I was afraid..."

"Which is understandable, by the way. Your mother wanted to be the one to call each of you, but was waiting for permission," Harlen continued. "She asked me to relay a message because she didn't want you finding out through the grapevine. She said to be strong and that if you need to speak to anyone, come see her."

More of that surprise struck.

"Said she's been in therapy and is working out at the gym now," Harlen said. "She doesn't want anyone to worry about her. In fact, she wants to be here for 'her boys' as she put it. But only if you want to see her."

"I-uh, I'm not sure how to respond to that," Kellan informed. "Of course, I want to see her. The next time you talk to her, tell her I'll be there as soon as I take care of something in Dallas."

"I'll communicate word back to Mrs. Firebrand on your behalf, Kellan," Sawyer promised.

"Much appreciated," Kellan responded. The prefix Mrs. caught his attention. Would she still be called that now? Or would she become Ms.? As silly as it might seem at this point, his brain still snapped to that question.

This was how it worked. The brain, as it tried to process shocking information, focused on these little points.

"Be safe out there," Sawyer said to Kellan.

"I plan to come home in one piece," Kellan promised. "And that's the reason I called."

He couldn't offer many details but said he needed accommodations for a couple of nights in the Dallas area near Loop 12.

"I'll have an address for you within the hour," Sawyer promised.

"Thank you," Kellan offered. "Not just for this but everything you've done for me and my family."

"It was and is my honor to serve the Firebrand family," Harlen stated with pride in his tone.

"You were the closest to my grandfather," Kellan continued. "More so than any of us."

"He had his issues," Harlen said. His voice cracked in a rare show of emotion. "But we were friends too."

"I know," Kellan said. "The Marshal was lucky to have you and so are we. Thank you for sticking around after his passing."

"I'll be here until I take my last breath," Harlen promised.

It was beyond Kellan how a man like his grandfather could have filled his life with such loyal and devoted people.

The man was complicated, and he left a complicated legacy.

"I'll call the others to tell them about Dad," Kellan said, his old instincts kicking in.

Harlen didn't immediately respond. Then came, "If I may say so, ever since you were a little boy, you've looked out for the other boys in the family. Being handed that kind of responsibility at such an early age isn't something most could handle. You were always too stubborn to quit. Your grandfather was proud of you and so was your father. But, Kellan, it's time to take care of yourself. Everyone else is okay. You don't have to worry anymore." Harlen paused. "I know that's easier said than done but you did right by the others."

"Is that why we've been bumping heads all these years?" he asked, touched by the speech even if he wasn't so certain he agreed with parts of it. Maybe the lawyer was right about one thing, though. His brothers were grown men with families of their own. They didn't need his protection anymore.

"You're talking about you and Adam," Harlen said. "Adam respects you, Kellan. He always has."

"That why he's been such a PITA?" Kellan was only half-joking.

"Adam wanted to be you for the longest time," Harlen said. "You were too young to remember this, but in kindergarten his teacher had the class dress up as their hero." Harlen paused. "Do you remember your favorite cowboy hat?"

"The one with the badge on it?" Kellan asked. "I sure do. Adam stole it and ended up losing the darn thing."

"He stole it because he dressed up as you that day in kindergarten," Harlen explained. "Everyone wanted to wear it, so it got passed around. Adam walked around with his chest puffed out all day until he lost track of the hat. Someone took it home and kept it."

"No way," Kellan said. Was that even possible?

"You and Adam had a fight about it, and have been fighting ever since, I guess," Harlen stated. "Your fathers got involved, and that only made it worse. Before that, the pair of you were inseparable."

Hells bells.

Didn't he feel like a jerk now?

"Why didn't anyone ever tell me this?" Kellan asked,

thinking it would have saved him a whole lifetime of butting heads with his cousin.

"What does the past matter?" Harlen asked. "The point is that you know now. What are you going to do with the information *now*?"

"I have no idea," Kellan answered honestly. "But I intend to figure it out."

"Stay tuned for the address," Harlen said, changing subjects after a thoughtful pause.

"Will do," Kellan said before ending the call.

Kelsey took one look at him. "Everything okay?" she asked.

"My father died today."

"Oh, Kellan," she said, her voice balm to a wounded soul. "I'm so sorry."

~

KELSEY CLIMBED over the console to sit in Kellan's lap. She wrapped her arms around his neck and just held on, like they were two people lost at sea in a raging storm with only each other to keep them from drowning.

She, of all people, knew what it was like to lose a father out of the blue. She, of all people, knew the shock of finding out. She, of all people, knew the regret of not being able to have one more conversation with that person to clear the air. To heal.

Kellan wrapped his arms around her like he was holding on for dear life too. They were two broken souls, fitting together in a perfect way.

She whispered words of comfort into his ear, wishing she could make things better. Knowing only time could heal wounds this deep.

Kelsey couldn't be certain how long they'd been in this position when his cell buzzed, but she could have stayed there forever.

He didn't immediately move. Neither seemed to want this moment to end. If only they could stay in this safe bubble for a while longer. Forever.

Kellan finally reached for the cell he'd placed in the cupholder. She started to move but he held onto her with his other arm. "Stay."

"Okay."

He checked the screen. There was an address. "No sleazy motel today. Okay?"

"Okay," she repeated.

After a few more minutes, she couldn't be certain how many, she shifted over to the passenger seat and buckled up. He gave her a look that sent fireballs of need rocketing through her, along with an ache she'd never felt before.

Loop 12 was interesting for the fact a liquor store with bars on the windows and crushed cigarette butts littering the ground was a two-block drive from one of the most expensive Dallas neighborhoods. University Park.

Kellan turned onto University Boulevard before finding the streets named after major universities. This University Boulevard, however, led to Southern Methodist University, or Southern Millionaire's University as some of the dancers at the club had called it. He made his way onto Amherst Avenue before parking in front of a two-story white brick with sea-green shudders. The new build, like others on this street, replaced forty-year-old original homes. This area had nice backyards and close proximity to Dallas. The trees were mature and it had a neighborhood feeling complete with sidewalks.

This was home to the Junior League ladies whose

husbands spent their lunch hour at places like Naked, Not Afraid. Kelsey had seen it firsthand. Before she worked in the club, she would have thought the clientele would be filthy construction workers who worked when they wanted to make enough money to hit the strip club or unkempt men who couldn't get a date. She'd been surprised to find lawyers and businessmen still in suits sitting beside construction workers and men who looked like they'd crawled out of a sewer to be there. Had she been naïve to think educated, sophisticated men went home to wives and children and never set foot in establishments like this? Yes. Growing up in a small town, mostly at church, had insulated her from reality. Then there were the Texas millionaires who had to be wheeled in because they were too old to stand up on their own two feet anymore. Celebrity Anna Nicole Smith should have tuned Kelsey in to those type of men but that was a long time ago, a special she'd once watched on TV while waiting for Jackson to come home.

Kelsey never would have believed in a million years that she would end up working in a place like Naked, Not Afraid, even as a waitress.

The tips had been good. Better than good. Money flowed in places like those. Dancers called themselves models. Clientele believed the dancers actually made a life choice to be there instead of ending up there after falling on hard times with no way out, the same as her. Or after living as runaways on the streets until reaching a hirable age.

Places like that were all smoke and mirrors, selling a fantasy.

Even while lost in thought, she noticed the minute Kellan turned into the University Park neighborhood where their next stop must be.

Talk about fantasy, the home on Amherst Avenue sold a lifestyle that Kelsey could only dream about.

Kellan pulled out front and parked the SUV on the street.

"Are we seriously going inside this home?" she asked him, stunned.

"Consider this home, sweet, home," he reassured before exiting the driver's side. He came around to her door, and then opened it too.

She took his hand, exited, and then leaned on him as he helped her to the front door. Two pots filled with greenery flanked the massive double doors. Kelsey leaned against one of them as Kellan checked the pots, one by one, for keys.

"We're in business," he said after checking the second pot. "Ready?"

"For a soft bed?" she asked before adding, "You have to be kidding if you need to ask that question."

Kellan's laugh was a low rumble in his chest. Sexy. But then, everything about him sent sensual shivers racing across her skin.

Inside the two-story white brick was just as impeccable as the manicured lawn.

"Five bedrooms and four and a half baths," Kellan said.

The place was light and bright, with enough touches of green to make Kelsey feel like she could be sitting in a garden. Of course, the finishes were top of the line too.

"This is a whole lot better than the motel I was taking us to," she said with a genuine smile. And then she laughed. She laughed at the absurdity of the situation. She laughed at everything life had thrown at her lately. She laughed because she was still alive to fight another day.

Every tide turned eventually. Would hers?

14

"Make yourself at home while I grab a shower," Kellan said to Kelsey. He would think more clearly after.

"Which bedroom is mine?" she asked with a hitch in her voice.

"Take the master," he said. "And I'll take one of the secondary bedrooms."

"Actually, since the other bedrooms are on the opposite side of the house, could you stay with me in the master?" she asked.

The bed was a California king so there was no threat of them touching. Not that he minded the idea of sleeping with arms and legs in a tangle with Kelsey, but they weren't a couple. He didn't need to become confused.

"Sure," he said. "It's safer that way."

His comment caused her lips to turn down at the corners in a slight frown. He hadn't intended to offend her with the comment. Rather than debate what she did or didn't want—because it might just be that she needed comfort and anyone would do—he grabbed the bag of supplies meant for him and headed toward the first floor master. Besides, when she'd been sitting on his lap in the SUV, he came dangerously close to thinking she belonged to him.

"Mind if I stick close?" Kelsey asked.

"Not at all," he responded, hearing the gravel-like quality to his own voice. What could he say? The thought of making love to Kelsey was a draw stronger than a magnet to steel. It would be a mistake, though. It would confuse the issue. He was there to help, not make matters worse for her. His emotions ran high after hearing the news about his father, which only served to muddy the waters. Because he could get lost in Kelsey. And he needed to stay focused.

A shower helped redirect his thoughts. Clean clothes were a miracle. Kelsey sat on the bed, then took over the bathroom to freshen up and change while he headed into the next room toward the fridge. Someone had been here recently. Were the occupants on vacation? He had no idea and no time to care. Harlen knew a whole lot of people. It shouldn't surprise Kellan that the lawyer had connections everywhere in the state.

Kellan's thoughts drifted to his family as he pulled out ingredients for sandwiches. He'd never been close to his father, but he understood what Kelsey said about the hollow feeling that comes with never being able to clear the air or make a relationship right before someone passed.

He also thought about his mother. Was the blow more difficult than she wanted to let on? Would she give up hope?

In their own ways, his parents did love each other. They'd spent a lifetime together. Although, his mother had been in her own world most of the time and his father had been absent. They stayed together, despite his mother's month-long trips to Houston, which had to mean something. And her drinking to numb the pain.

If nothing else, they'd shared nine children together. Kellan could barely think about having one or two little ones running around after being around the new kids in the fold, let alone nine. Had his parents been in over their heads?

Unquestionably yes.

At this point, though, letting the past impact his future seemed silly. Kellan had spent too much time angry at his parents, at the world. It was time to let go. Everyone in the family was married, some with kids or kids on the way. Everyone was an adult who was capable of living life on their own terms. Kellan had spent so much of his time worrying about everyone else that he'd forgotten how to live. Damn. The realization zapped him with the force of a stray lightning bolt. After exiting the bathroom, he met Kelsey in the bedroom where she waited, curled on her side on the bed.

"You must be starving," he said to her as he helped her up. "Do you want to wait here while I fix something to eat?" Living on his own had made him decent in the kitchen. In no time, he'd put together some sandwiches from the ingredients he'd pulled from the fridge, plated them, and put on coffee.

"I don't want to be alone right now," she admitted in a rare, vulnerable moment. "Mind if I become your shadow?"

"I'll help you up," he said, but she waved him off.

"I got this." Kelsey stood up and followed him into the kitchen, hopping on her good foot. "I forgot there are supplies in here to wrap this thing." She motioned toward her ankle.

"Sit down while I grab the medical kit," he said after

pulling out a chair in the corner of the room where there was a round table with four chairs next to a window. He crossed the room so she could lean on him to get to the seat.

Then, he grabbed the bag with medical supplies in it.

At least he wasn't worried about the SUV fitting in this neighborhood. There was a sea of SUVs and Range Rovers lining the street out front. Theirs wouldn't cause anyone to perform a double take.

Hiding in plain sight.

"Do the other waitresses at the club know your situation?" he asked as he returned to the kitchen and took a knee. He set the bag down next to him and then searched inside for medical gauze. Found it. This was the kind that didn't need extra adhesive.

"Not specifically, no," she said. "But that doesn't mean they couldn't figure it out in the general sense. Everyone working there has a story."

He cocked an eyebrow as he focused on the grapefruit size ankle on an otherwise slim, runner's leg.

"What I mean is that no one works there because they have a trust fund to fall back on," she said.

It was his turn to wince.

"I didn't mean you," she offered with an awkward smile.

He shook it off. But maybe now she could see why he would feel the need to make his own way in the world.

"What I meant to say before I put my foot in my mouth was—"

"You couldn't," he interrupted.

"What?"

"Put your foot in your mouth," he quipped with a grin. "It wouldn't fit with that ankle."

Kelsey laughed. He laughed.

Laughter had been rare. It felt good. It broke some of the

tension they both felt being this close to a confrontation with the men who were after her, not to mention the electrical current that ran between the two of them.

"Fine," she said with a playful tap on his shoulder.

He caught her hand and brought her wrist to his lips before feathering a kiss there. Her arm goosebumped. Rather than let himself get caught up in wanting what he couldn't have, he dropped her hand and got back to work on her ankle.

She recovered quickly, sitting up a little straighter. "No one works a place like Naked, Not Afraid without a backstory, and probably a sad one, because even as strip clubs go, it's not somewhere you'd choose to work. I overheard some of the dancers talk. They suffered abuse at the hands of various men. You wouldn't think that would lead to a life of topless dancing but apparently it can. I asked one of the dancers once and she told me that if men were going to objectify her, she wanted to be in control." She shook her head. "I guess that's how they survive what happened to them."

"Breaks your heart to think that's someone's sister or daughter up there on those stages," he said after a thoughtful pause.

"You can see why I wouldn't want news of me taking a job in one of those places to get back to my parents," she said. "It would only make them condemn me more and feel like failures in a bigger way. They couldn't help me out of my financial trouble if they'd wanted to and I know that would bother any parent."

"You did what you had to in order to survive," he reiterated. "That makes you a survivor and pretty damn strong in my book."

"Ever just get tired of being strong?"

"Yes," he admitted with a sharp sigh and no hesitation.

"Thank you for not making me feel weak for admitting that," she said, catching his gaze with those violet eyes that seemed to see right through him.

Kellan forced his gaze back onto her ankle before he got himself in trouble again, wishing for something that wasn't going to happen. Couldn't happen. Shouldn't happen?

Then again, he was getting damn tired of fighting his feelings for Kelsey. When this was over, he could play the *what if* game. *What if* she moved back to Lone Star Pass? *What if* she didn't? *What if* they tried long distance dating?

Right now, he needed to focus on keeping both of them alive long enough to put the bastards after her behind bars for the rest of their lives.

~

GETTING USED to Kellan's touch would do Kelsey no good, so she focused on something else instead. How were they going to walk into the club? Through the front doors? Through the dancer's entrance in the back?

"One of the other waitresses must know something more about the men after me," she reasoned, steering the conversation back on track.

"If others have done favors, they might," Kellan said, glancing at the clock. He finished taping up her ankle and then took a seat at the table. "We have a couple of hours before the club will be hopping." He motioned toward the sandwiches. "That'll give us plenty of time to eat, rest, and come up with a plan."

"My thoughts exactly," she agreed.

"Any chance I can get you to take ibuprofen?" he continued.

"Normally, no," she said. "But right now, I need to get on top of this pain."

"Ice doesn't help much with swelling," Kellan stated as he grabbed a couple of tablets out of the medical bag his lawyer had put together. "Folks are finally figuring that out."

She remembered the doctor saying something about it helping to numb the injury. "A high ankle sprain will take its time healing."

"Not much you can do," he agreed before setting the tablets down on her plate. Next, he brought over a glass of water and set it down. "Best to eat before you take those."

She did as he filled mugs before joining her.

The sandwiches hit the spot. The cup of coffee after almost made her feel like they were a normal couple living in a dream home together about to raise a family.

Kelsey was pushing forty. Was a family even realistic?

Sure, there were procedures and hormones. But would she be able to conceive naturally?

She shook the thought off. Facing the possibility of death was doing strange things to her mind. She'd resigned herself to never having kids a long time ago.

"I'll do dishes," Kellan said when their plates were clean.

"That doesn't seem fair," she argued. "You made food. I should be on clean-up duty."

"As soon as your ankle is better, I'll take you up on that," he said, like they had some kind of future together beyond tonight. For one thing, they had to show up at the club and then live to tell about it. For another, they had to commit to seeing each other again. Both seemed far out of reach at this point. "In the meantime, let's get some rest."

"Deal." As she tried to force herself to stand, Kellan appeared by her side. He swept her up off her feet and carried her to the bed before she could muster a good protest. "Stay with me."

Kellan helped her under the covers before joining her. She settled into the crook of his arm and drifted off.

The next couple of hours went by in a flash. Before Kelsey knew—or was ready for that matter—it was time to wake up.

She sat up and rubbed her eyes, immediately noticing the empty spot where Kellan had been. As she tried to shake off the sleep fog, he appeared in the doorway, holding two mugs. Heaven?

"I tried to get back before you woke up," he said with the kind of smile that would melt a thousand hearts. Hers was no exception.

"You might be too good to be true," she said, taking one of the mugs with fresh brew.

He turned on the light and joined her, sitting on the edge of the bed. "I'm no angel."

"I'm counting on it," she teased, appreciating the break in tension. The thought of going back to the club made her skin crawl. Bringing Kellan along embarrassed her. It was one thing to hear about someone's bad luck but to see it firsthand was something else altogether.

Would he see her differently once they were inside her former workplace?

After coffee, Kelsey was about to find out.

∼

LIGHTS from the club's sign illuminated this stretch of the otherwise dark road. Naked, Not Afraid came alive at night. The parking lot was full. There were plenty of trucks and luxury vehicles. It looked like a dealership with how many late-model Audis and Range Rovers filled the spots.

Being back here made Kelsey sick in the pit of her stomach.

Kellan found a spot away from the building and parked. "We can hop the curb if need be for a quick getaway."

"We might need it," she said.

He exited the SUV and came around to her side of the vehicle as she opened the door. He helped her down.

She tested the ankle by putting a little weight on it. The tape was tight enough that she could put weight on it if she had to. Best not to push it, though.

"Is it feeling any better?" Kellan asked as they walked across the gravel parking lot.

"Some," she said. "I won't be running any marathons but it's definitely not worse off."

He smiled and nodded.

"It's likely I'll be recognized the minute we step inside the door," she said to Kellan. "Be prepared."

"Always," he reassured.

As they made it to the front door, music pulsing, the bouncer named Teddy opened the door from inside. He took one look at Kelsey and his face washed of color.

"That's not good," she said under her breath.

Teddy stepped out and scanned the area. "What are you doing back here?"

"She's fine," Kellan instantly stepped in between her and Teddy, blocking his access.

"It's okay," she said to Kellan. Teddy was the one who'd gotten her the fake ID in the first place. He was just being protective. "I'm back."

The bouncer's head was already shaking. "Not good, Kels. You gotta get outta here."

"I was followed, Teddy."

The big man's expression morphed to fear. "Go while you still can," he said. "Use the ID I got you. Get out of the country for a while until things cool down."

"Who is behind this?" she asked, figuring he must have an idea.

Teddy shook his head. "Wouldn't do any good to tell you if I knew."

"Why me?" she asked. "Why did they pick me?"

"You seriously haven't figured it out yet?" the familiar voice came from behind.

Kellan whirled around, tucking her behind him. "Jackson? What the hell do you have to do with this?"

Jackson's gaze bounced from Kellan's to Kelsey's and back. "What's he doing here, Kels?"

"He's with me," she quipped, hating the nickname when Jackson said it. "And that's none of your business anymore."

"It is when you screw up a deal for me," Jackson stated. He brought his hand up to reveal a gun. "Where's the damn box?"

"What?" Kelsey could scarcely believe those words. "You?"

"Who do you think was behind the choice to pick you, for God's sake?" Jackson asked. "Look, this was supposed to help get us both out of the hole until you screwed it up. Time is running out, Kels. If we don't get that box back to..." Jackson involuntarily shivered.

"What made you so certain that I would run this errand in the first place?" she asked, stalling so Kellan could figure out a plan.

Jackson's face morphed to pure evil. Eyes that once sparkled with excitement for a future were nothing but slate. "Everyone put your hands up," Jackson warned. "I need to see 'em." There was a hysterical quality to his tone and his eyes were wild. He was right about one thing, though. They were both in trouble now.

"Don't do this," Kellan warned but Jackson looked right past him to her.

"Step off, asshole," Jackson responded without making eye contact with Kellan. The man was intent on Kelsey. The way he looked at her caused icy fingers to grip her spine. "I just need you to come with me, take me to the box, and then no one will get hurt," Jackson said, his voice a little too desperate for her liking. Desperate people did desperate things.

"What if I refuse?" she asked.

Jackson shifted the barrel to the center of Kellan's chest. "Then your boyfriend here gets blown away. Is that what you want?"

"No. No. No." Panic gripped her. "Don't do that, Jackson. Don't point that thing at anyone. It might go off."

"That's the point, Kels," Jackson stated, his voice on the verge of losing it. She'd heard it too many times to ignore it now. "If I go down, I'm taking your boyfriend down with me. How about that?"

"Haven't you taken enough from me?" she responded, trying to keep her voice as level as possible despite the white-hot anger coursing through her veins.

"Why couldn't you just do this one thing right?" Jackson bemoaned. "You'll take us both down, when you were supposed to be my ticket out of this shitstorm."

Then, he squeezed the trigger.

15

Kellan dove to the ground, taking Kelsey along with him. The second they hit gravel, he rolled on top of her to shield her with his body. Teddy drew down on Jackson as another shot was fired. This time, the shot hit its target. Blood squirted from Teddy's neck. An artery?

Jesus.

The bouncer came down on his knees first as he grabbed at the hole in his neck. Trying to plug it up was the equivalent of covering the tip of a firehose with a mason jar lid.

Kellan's instinct to go to the injured person had to be quashed. Instead, he gathered Kelsey up with one arm and used the other to help crawl on his knees behind a truck in the parking lot, holding her tight to his chest.

The gun noise should draw attention. Kellan needed to keep Kelsey hidden long enough for help to arrive.

Then again, the loud volume of music inside the club would drown out everything else.

Someone had to show up or leave, though. The door

bouncer was down. How long would it take someone on the inside to figure it out? Was there someone working the door besides Teddy? A hostess?

The bouncer would have been the one to intervene and call for help. How long before someone noticed Teddy was missing?

"Stay down," Kellan whispered to Kelsey, wishing he had a better idea than to slide underneath a truck. All Jackson had to do was drop down on all fours to find them. He'd fired twice, proving he wasn't afraid to shoot. The man was panicked and desperate, a bad combination for those around him who wanted to stay alive.

Kellan wriggled in the rocks—their points digging into the flesh of his forearm—enough to hide most of their bodies behind the wheels.

"That sonofabitch," Kelsey said low and under her breath. "Did he wrangle one of his new bandmates to follow me? Run me off the road? Was that him all along?"

The sound of footsteps caused him to slide in between her and the shuffle of feet, heading toward them.

"Roll that way," Kellan urged, nudging her to move away from the direction of the footsteps. With her bad ankle, she wouldn't be able to run. Their SUV was too far away. They would never make it in time as trigger happy as Jackson turned out to be. The delusional man would shoot until he hit his target. Unless he ran out of ammo. Somehow, Kellan believed the man was prepared for war.

Teddy lay there, bleeding out. Kellan had never felt so helpless in his life.

Could he draw attention away from Kelsey long enough for her to get inside the SUV and drive away? Then, make it to Teddy before he bled to death?

"Take this," he whispered, shoving the key fob in her

hand. "Don't press the button to unlock the SUV until your hand is on the door handle. Okay?"

"No," she protested.

"We don't have time to debate," he countered. "He wants you, not me."

Kelsey opened her mouth to argue but seemed to think better of it. He wasn't kidding. Time was the enemy.

"Stay hidden behind the vehicles and lean on them to help you walk," he instructed. Before she could argue, he rolled opposite and hopped to his feet, staying in a crouched position.

Kellan rounded the back of the truck and then moved down. He slammed into a random truck's hood, causing its alarm to pierce the air, drawing attention away from Kelsey.

The more noise he made, the better.

He moved over several vehicles, staying low, and did the same thing. And then repeated the action several more times until the night air was full of the ear-piercing noises. This way, Jackson wouldn't be able to tell when Kelsey hit the unlock button for the SUV as Kellan drew the gunman away from her.

This was still a risk. But Kellan lacked a better plan.

Now, he needed to locate Jackson and surprise the bastard from behind. Kellan dropped down to all fours as the doors to the club slammed open and customers flooded the exit. Kellan was able to see someone immediately rush to Teddy's aid to the backdrop of a cacophony of ear-piercing sirens.

Jackson could get away. And then what?

Kelsey would have to spend days, weeks, or months looking over her shoulder? Never knowing when her ex might show up?

Kellan couldn't allow that to happen.

Damn that he'd split them up.

He popped his head up long enough to check for the SUV. It was still there in the same spot it had been parked in.

Fear struck. His chest tightened. Panic gripped him. Had Jackson gotten to Kelsey?

∼

KELSEY HOPPED ON ONE FOOT, key fob in hand, trying to figure out how to get out of this mess with Kellan and figure out a way to help Teddy. The SUV was four vehicles away. Based on the car alarms, Kellan was on the other side of the parking lot by now.

His plan was smart. She hoped it would work.

Waiting to the last minute to click the button, she craned her neck to see if the coast was clear.

It was.

She hit the button a second after her hand gripped the door handle.

Half expecting Jackson to appear, nerves on fire, she opened the door and then managed to hop into the driver's seat. The second her bottom touched leather, she slammed the door behind her. Should she lock the doors? Or would Kellan appear out of seemingly nowhere and need immediate access?

One thing was certain, she wasn't leaving this parking lot without him. Period.

Was the windshield bulletproof?

She had no idea if vehicles were made to withstand shooters these days as standard equipment. She'd never needed to know.

Hell, she was still trying to wrap her mind around the

fact Jackson had been the one to set her up on this errand. Had he been following her? Keeping tabs on her?

A few details in her brain clicked. Like how he seemed to know the days she got in late from work when they were married. At the time, he'd said he had a sixth sense, a connection, and she'd bought his lies.

They say you see yourself in what you notice in others. Kelsey had covered up her life when it came to her parents but she was an honest person. She expected others to be honest. While in survival mode, she hadn't picked up the signs Jackson was a lying bastard.

He was good at it, though.

Had he sent someone to kill her in order to make amends to the men he'd signed up to help? Or had the fire in the shed been meant to flush her out of hiding? Doing away with her?

More questions flooded her. Should she start the engine? With all the noise, it shouldn't give her away. Should she wait for Kellan? He'd said to leave but how could she go without him? More than that, where would she go? Back to the house?

She couldn't see herself doing that without Kellan and while Teddy was dying.

Hanging around being a sitting duck wasn't the move. Kelsey had waited long enough. She didn't have it in her to wait any longer.

Rather than start the engine, she exhaled sharply and exited the SUV.

The parking lot was filling with clientele in a hurry to get the hell out of here before the cops showed up. She could use the flurry of activity as a distraction.

Moving toward the door of the club, she immediately

saw that Teddy was surrounded by men who were administering aid. Doctors?

It wouldn't surprise her. The club had clientele from every walk of life and this group looked like it knew what it was doing.

Would Jackson run? Hide?

There were no new vehicle sirens, so she moved toward the area of the last one. How long had it been? A minute? Longer? Time seemed to slow down in stressful situations. Life moved in frames rather than real-time.

And then out of the corner of her eye, she saw Jackson's back. Kellan was standing five feet away from him. Based on the way Jackson looked from behind, he was lifting his gun toward Kellan.

Adrenaline coursed through her at the sight. Kelsey couldn't allow Kellan to die. The thought of living on this earth without him...

She couldn't go there. Not when she'd finally found him again.

So, she bolted toward Jackson—ankle be damned—and then let out a cat-like screech as she launched herself onto his back. A shot rang out.

Using her nails as claws, she dug into Jackson's eyes as he violently tried to shake her off.

Not today, asshole. Kelsey hung on for dear life, focusing all her energy on slapping the gun out of his hand. She had no idea if the bullet hit its mark and couldn't risk a glance for fear she would give Jackson the advantage.

He bent forward. She managed to wrap one of her legs around his midsection. Using her heel, she dug into the spot no man wanted a heel. Despite the loud sirens, she heard Jackson bite out a curse.

The pain caused him to drop to his knees. Kelsey went flying onto the hard gravel. Her head slammed into a tire.

Frantic, her gaze flew to Kellan as he launched himself toward Jackson.

Fists flew but Jackson was no match for Kellan physically. Within a few seconds, Kellan was on top of Jackson, pinning his arms to his sides using powerful thighs.

"Help," Kelsey shouted for anyone to hear, as she moved to get the gun that had been knocked out of Jackson's hand.

By the time she got to it, cops surrounded them. She put her hands in the air as, one by one, sirens were silenced. The parking lot was half empty by now. Although, she could barely see much else in the dust cloud. From here, though, she witnessed Teddy being loaded into the back of an ambulance.

"Will Teddy survive?" she immediately asked the cop nearest to her.

"It looks like help arrived in time," the cop responded before taking her statement. She told them everything. She told them about the weapons in the storage facility. She gave them the address. She told them where to find the box of guns. And she told them about her ex setting her up.

One of the other cops took Kellan's place holding down Jackson while Kelsey was giving her statement. The lawman locked Jackson's hands behind his back in cuffs as Kellan gave his statement. Witnesses corroborated their stories, so they were given the go-ahead to leave once it was all said and done, and Jackson was loaded into the back of a cruiser.

Kellan carried Kelsey to the SUV, unlocked the door, and gently placed her inside.

"I kept expecting the police to break out the handcuffs on me for stealing the car at the hospital," she said to Kellan.

He checked his phone. "You can read it for yourself but Sheriff Lawler called Harlen to forward a message from the owner of the vehicle. She's a retired schoolteacher who was doing volunteer work at the hospital. She wanted to thank us for the cabin. Turns out her five-year-old grandson loves to fish and her husband is already busy making plans for weekend barbecues."

Kellan's kindness touched her heart. "That's amazing."

"You're amazing," he countered.

"Where do we go from here?" she asked, thankful the former schoolteacher would have such a beautiful place to make memories with her family.

Kellan's expression morphed as he looked at her. "I lost you once. Let you slip right out of my hands. I don't want to do that a second time. Being with you has shown me what I forgot along the way...what true love feels like. I know we haven't been back together for long and the circumstances have been...intense for lack of a better word. Life throws a lot of curves and speedbumps. But I'm sure of one thing. I've loved you since we were juniors in high school. I just didn't know what the feeling meant back then. I'm in love with you now. And, if you'll have me, I want to spend the rest of my life with you, loving you, taking care of you." He took in a slow breath. "What do you think, Kelsey? Will you be my partner in life? Will you stay with me this time?"

"I'll do more than that, Kellan," she said with the biggest smile and fullest heart. "I'll marry you."

Kelsey could finally come home again. Home meant anywhere with Kellan Firebrand, the man she could never seem to forget or never stop loving.

"I love you," he said to her, sending warmth through her.

"I've loved you most of my life," she replied, wondering

if she'd ever truly loved anyone else. "Do you think it's too late to start a family?"

"I hope not," Kellan said with a smile that sent warmth through her. The way he looked at her...this was love. Real love. And she loved him right back. "But biology is only one way. There are others."

"Okay then," she said. "How soon can we start?"

His grin made him even more handsome. "Now too soon?"

And then he kissed her so tenderly it robbed her breath. After all these years, she could finally go home.

16

EPILOGUE

Three years later.

THE SMELL OF GINGER, cinnamon, and sugar filled the expansive kitchen. Kellan took in the scene he would never have believed possible most of his life. Baby Angel wasn't such a baby anymore. Kellan had heard the term 'terrific twos and even better threes' bantered around, which he liked better than hearing 'terrible twos and even worse threes.' It should be the family mantra at this point. It was only a matter of months before Angel would be in the clear, her parents free of battles for independence and tantrums. Adam and Prudence were good parents to Angel. The baby on the way was going to be a lucky kid to have a big sister and loving parents.

Kellan's kid still walked like a drunk. At eighteen months, baby Adam was equal part brave and idiot. The kid learned to walk by throwing himself toward his mother at ten months old from across the room, giving an amusing new meaning to the term *Look before you leap*.

Kelsey amazed Kellan. Seeing her hold their child in her arms for the first time flipped a switch inside him. One that overwhelmed him with unconditional love. He was the luckiest man alive and knew it.

Brax and Raleigh sat at the large wood table, talking with Dane and Catalina. Raleigh's country music career hit high gear after releasing The Loft, a song written from the loft of one of the Firebrand barns. Raleigh had asked Kelsey to sing backup vocals on her next album, to which his wife had happily agreed. His mother-in-law sat at the table, chatting away with the others in the family. Life was good.

"When does your tour end?" Catalina asked Raleigh. She'd worked wonders with the Firebrand computer network, putting her software developer skills to good use.

Raleigh's hand dropped to her stomach. "In two months. Then, we're home in the studio for a year." She glanced at her husband, Brax. Kellan could have sworn he saw her face flush. What was that about?

Dane and Catalina had been secretive about their plans to have a family, but Kellan suspected the baby craze was hitting them too. He expected an announcement to come any day now.

The back door opened. Miss Peabody, a sweet bichon, and Hutch, a Labrador retriever, came blasting through, causing the usual flurry of excitement.

Baby Adam's grin was ear-to-ear. He started toward Hutch. Kelsey immediately picked him up before he could be knocked on his backside. Hutch was large enough to ride. Although, everyone here knew better than to put a child on his back. He might be large but he was no horse. Besides, the barn was full of those.

Prudence shot over, trying to rally the dogs before one of the kids got knocked over.

Romy and Eric came rushing in behind the dogs, apologizing for letting them in without advanced warning.

"It's fine," said a chorus of voices. Everyone in this house loved animals and there were plenty of them running around. If they added more, they'd have to apply for a zoo license.

Romy had been forced to spy on the Firebrand business, but she and Eric had fallen in love and she couldn't follow through with the plot against the family. She'd come to work at Firebrand and proved a valuable asset.

One thing was certain, life was always shifting. There was no use trying to stand still. Better to shift with the changes.

"Merry Christmas, everyone," Eric said, taking in the room. His and Romy's arms were full of packages. "Can anyone help unload the truck? Romy went a little overboard this year."

Kellan laughed. Everyone did. To the point, the front room wasn't much more than a Christmas tree and presents stacked a mile high with a small path carved out so the chairs could be reached.

Fallon jumped up, gave his wife Birdie a kiss, and followed Eric outside. Brax and a couple others followed while Birdie stayed next to her beloved grandmother.

"When will Grayson and Kyra get here?" Prudence asked her husband, Adam.

As if on cue, the front door opened and their voices could be heard as they made their way down the hallway to the kitchen. Kyra was modern-day royalty but part cowgirl when she came home to the ranch with Grayson.

"Where do the presents go?" Kyra asked after another

chorus of Merry Christmas rang out along with hugs. Kyra might look fragile but she was as bad-ass as they came, having learned martial arts with her cousin from a young age. Turned out that her father always feared a takeover plot and didn't want Kyra defenseless. She could hold her own in conversation, keeping Grayson on his toes.

Luis and Luna came bolting down the long hallway. The Dobermans belonged to Henry, who was now on the cusp of being a teenager. Ian and Daphne's son was growing up to be a fine young man.

All the little kids, affectionately called The Ankle Biters, bum-rushed Henry, knocking him a few steps back into the wall. Henry's smile matched the ones on the Biters.

Hudson and Anisa had a young one.

Katy came waddling into the kitchen, belly full with twins that were due in a couple of months. Vaughn fussed over his wife, making certain she had everything she wanted and needed. Kellan had never seen his brother more attentive. He and Katy had come a long way after breaking up in high school and now. Her uncle's intervention had brought the two back together and they'd been inseparable ever since. It warmed Kellan's heart.

Speaking of true love, Rafe and Odette were living proof love came in all shapes and sizes. The right fit wasn't always the obvious choice. But when something worked, it worked. In order to protect her younger sister, Odette took a job as a surrogate. Rafe lost the love of his life when Emile died. Finding out they had embryos meant having the family they'd always wanted. Falling in love with the surrogate gave Rafe a second chance at true love.

Kellan smiled at his younger brother. Rafe had been to hell and back. Here he was, still standing. Finding love. And having the family he was meant to have all along. He and

Odette adopted her younger sibling, giving Henry someone closer in age to help handle and play with the Biters.

Avril and Morgan sat at the table, holding hands after Morgan returned from helping bring in presents.

Nick, Morgan's twin, lost out on his high school sweetheart when her high-powered career father had other plans for Vanessa. She was to become a lawyer, not a rancher's wife. He'd intervened, breaking the young couple apart. True love brought them back together when Kellan's mom reached out to Vanessa's law firm for representation. Now that Vanessa's last name was Firebrand, representing Jackie Firebrand would be a conflict of interest so the young lawyer pulled strings and now Jackie was represented by the best criminal defense team in Texas.

"Where's Rowan and Tara?" Nick asked Adam, who was taking it all in and watching the kids interact with a wide smile on his face.

"They're on the way," Adam responded. He checked the clock. "Should be here any minute."

Kellan couldn't imagine fitting more presents in the front room. He also couldn't help but think about all the missed Christmases in this home. The Marshal could have given the Grinch a run for his money. All this space and yet there'd been no laughter in the hallways. There'd been no big family Christmases or any other holiday. No birthdays celebrated, not even the Marshal's.

What a waste.

The back door opened. Aimee and Tanner walked in, bundles of presents stacked so high it was next to impossible to see their faces. They were young. They had time before starting a family. And yet, Kellan was certain he'd seen that twinkle in Aimee's eyes while playing with the kids over Thanksgiving.

Speaking of babies, Keith and Amaya were still in their twenties. They were loving life, loving each other, and traveling. An online influencer, Amaya's reputation might have been restored but she worked behind the scenes now for Raleigh's band. As it turned out, promoting others gave Amaya the freedom she craved to be out of the spotlight.

Amaya sat next to Raleigh, the two engaged in cheerful banter.

Travis and Brynne walked in next, coming from the front door. Their daughter immediately did the noodle-thing toddlers seemed to have mastered so she could get out of her mother's arms to play.

Another round of Merry Christmases rang out as each new person or couple found their way to the kitchen.

Brynne's mother was next. It had been three years since her Parkinson's diagnosis. She was responding to treatment, which was giving her more precious time.

Time, Kellan realized, caught up to everyone. It was more important than money, coming in a close second to good health, without which time mattered less.

Damn if he wasn't getting philosophical in his old age. In actuality, having baby Adam had shifted Kellan's perspective the most. Babies held a special magic. They brought people together. They made room for forgiveness and selflessness.

If Kellan could bottle whatever it was they had, the world would be a better place.

Callie, a.k.a. Callie-Bell, had changed Travis's life for the better despite the surprise pregnancy that turned into a huge blessing for his brother. He and Brynne made an amazing team on her farm. She'd given a couple of her regular, dependable workers a piece of the action so she could learn more of the business, make more profits to share. The experiment worked. Travis split his time between the farm and family cattle ranch.

It worked.

Bronc Harris entered through the back door next. He was just as much a part of this family as anyone, along with Aunt Lucia. Baby Adam would never know his grandfather but the kid was surrounded by love.

Kellan looked around. Competition, anger, and hatred went to the grave with his father and uncle. Both had come to their senses a little too late. They'd apologized to each in their own way, trying to make peace with their children. Neither lived long enough to experience the results.

In some small way, Kellan believed in his heart that the brothers were together, laughing, maybe fishing, and finally at peace.

Adam made his way next to Kellan, leaning against the same counter.

"When does Aunt Jackie move to house arrest?" Adam asked.

"Not until after the holidays, I'm afraid," Kellan informed. His mother had been attacked twice without provocation while in prison, badly beaten both times. Prison wasn't safe for her.

"I had an idea that I wanted to run past you before we brought it to the group," Adam said.

"Okay, what gives?"

"I don't know why I didn't see it before, but Prudence pointed out that we moved into this house without ever asking your side of the family if it was okay," Adam said, his face twisting in regret.

"You didn't have to," Kellan pointed out, despite agreeing with Prudence.

"What you have to do and what is right to do can be two different things," Adam responded.

Kellan nodded. "What are you suggesting then?"

"This place is too big for my family," Adam said. "We're building an addition to my original home. So, I thought maybe your mom might want to take it over. I know my mom has been lonely ever since Dad died. She's been visiting your mom on a regular basis. What do you think about offering this place to them instead? Your mom could own the deed."

A wide smile planted itself on Kellan's face. "I can't think of a better idea, except to say they should share the deed. After everything the two of them have been through, they deserve to be treated as equals."

"Our fathers missed the boat on that one, didn't they?" Adam asked, but the question was rhetorical.

Kellan agreed. "It's time to reverse the curse, don't you think?"

"I do," Adam said before the two embraced in a bear hug.

From the corner of Kellan's eye, he saw Angel rip a toy out of baby Adam's hands. His son opened his mouth, winding up to cry.

Parental protection instincts kicked in, causing Kellan to want to storm over. His temper flared. His hands fisted. But then Henry, who'd watched the scene unfold, put an arm around both kids. Whatever he said in the huddle must have worked because Angel returned the toy, said she was sorry, and kissed baby Adam.

Then, she wiped away crocodile tears spilling out of baby Adam's eyes, rolling down his cheeks.

Kellan glanced over at his cousin, whose jaw had

dropped as he witnessed the scene unfolding. Kellan was still trying to pick his own up from the floor.

"I'll go over there and reprimand her if you say," Adam offered.

"There's no need," Kellan reassured. "The kids are handling the situation fine on their own."

Just then, baby Adam wrapped his cherub arms around Angel. All was forgiven. They were best pals again.

"Leave it to the babes to light the way," Adam said under his breath.

Kellan couldn't agree more.

Time was fleeting. Before he knew it, these babies would be the adults standing in the room watching their children play and interact. A whole new generation of Firebrands were already walking these halls. Change was in the air. It was about time.

And it was good.

∽

IF YOU ENJOYED THE FIREBRANDS, **here's an excerpt from another series I think you'll love:**

REGINA ANDERSON TUCKED her earbuds in, tied off her running shoes, and pushed off her front porch. She turned up the volume on the heavy metal rock band music she played. Mornings sucked. Running sucked. Loud music sucked. The ritual kept Gina, as everyone but her mother called her, from taking her anger out on the world.

The loose, wet gravel on the drive of the fishing cabin caused her foot to slip as she rounded the corner onto the familiar country road. A couple extra forward steps righted her as she struggled to find her pace. Those first few steps were always the hardest to take, she reminded herself. Nothing in her wanted to do this.

The morning air didn't help matters. With every breath, she felt the crisp edge to the frigid temperature burning her lungs. The simple act of taking in oxygen was the equivalent to painful stabs at her rib cage.

Gina pounded the pavement with her feet. The stress of a major move with a baby, even though she was moving back to the small town where she'd grown up, had given her a tension headache.

It was early. Six a.m. was an ungodly hour.

Head throbbing, what she really wanted was caffeine. Big cup. Quiet room. The quiet room was a fantasy once her daughter, Everly, woke, but the coffee was realistic.

The sun beat down on a spot at the crown of Gina's head. April weather in Gunner, Texas, was unpredictable. Today, the sun was out and the temperature was expected to hover around forty-seven degrees. This time of year, days could be swallowed up with thunderstorms and the kind of lightning that raced sideways for miles across a dark sky. Much like the thunderstorm from last night, but Gina didn't mind. That kind of weather matched her mood.

At twenty-seven years old, she was a single mom to a little girl who would never know her father, a man who'd been so anxious for his daughter's arrival he'd painted her room pink the day a sonogram revealed her sex. Little did Gina know it would be the last day she'd ever see her husband again. Their daughter, Everly, would never meet her father.

The music matched the level of her anger at losing a decent man who would've been a great father. The things she would go back and do differently if she could. The regret that filled her chest and hardened her heart toward the world, but not towards Everly, was heavier today.

Bright sunny days just soured her. The run gave her a sense of normalcy in a world that had turned upside down. She'd stayed in Dallas for the rest of her pregnancy; bringing her baby home to the house she'd shared with Des had been important to her. After all the work he'd done on the nursery, she wanted baby Everly to spend her first year there. It only seemed right to Gina, a small way to honor Des.

Gina's mother had put up a strong argument for her to move home to Gunner so she would have help with the baby. Gina loved her mother, don't get her wrong, the woman was a saint in many ways. But she just hadn't been ready to love her mother full-time. Mom was a little too free with advice about pretty much every aspect of life and a little too needy when it came to attention.

Growing up, it had only been Gina and her parents. There'd been no siblings or cousins around, no extended family. Gina had always wondered what it would be like to be surrounded by a large family. Big holiday gatherings with all the trimmings. Boisterous laughter around a table brimming with every food a kid could imagine. Kids running around wild and happy. Her parents had been busy with the restaurant, or too tired from it to do anything but relax after work, and so she'd been left to her own devices for much of her childhood.

Mom had been right about one thing, though. Everly needed as much family to surround her as possible, even if it was down to an overbearing mother and her friends.

Thinking about the piles of unopened boxes lining the walls of the family's cabin on the lake, Gina already felt defeated. She would get there, she reminded herself on almost an hourly basis. It had become her mantra.

The boxes would eventually be unpacked. She'd make the two-bedroom cabin feel like home. It might take some time, especially considering she had a little one to care for and was starting right in with the family restaurant tomorrow, but the work would get done. It always did.

It was good to remind herself of her other favorite mantra in moments like these. Chin up. Smile on. Power through. God, she was so damn tired from 'powering through' the past year-and-a-half.

Plus, she'd always planned to come back and take over the family business at some point. It's what her mother had done. And her grandmother before that. The restaurant had been operating in Gunner for three generations already. Gina would be number four, and she hoped Everly would want to carry on the tradition someday. But only if she wanted to. Gina wouldn't force her daughter into a life she didn't want.

For Gina, the restaurant gave her a connection to family. There was so little of that left. Another benefit now that she was a single mother came in the form of extra time with her daughter. A breakfast-only job would make Gina more available to Everly and after losing Des so suddenly, she was never more aware of just how precious time could be.

Those thoughts were too heavy for this early in the morning. She cranked up the volume but even the loud drum banging and screech of a metal guitar couldn't distract her today. She hated days like this where missing Des was an ache. There were too many days she didn't want to get out of bed. In times like these she felt the dark clouds hanging over her head might never clear.

The sun comes out in every season, even spring. How

many times had her mother repeated the mantra? It obviously gave her mother great comfort. For Gina, not so much. The only bright spot in Gina's past year was asleep in a crib while her new babysitter hovered.

Gina rounded the corner onto a country road and finally hit her stride. At least her run was working for her this morning. The runner's high kicked in, temporarily abating her need for a caffeine IV, although she wouldn't turn one down. The move had brought on plenty of additional stress. Then there was leaving her job—a job that had been her lifeline in recent months.

The heavy metal band, RockSlam, pounded her ears, penetrating her thoughts, numbing her. A half hour into her run and it had finally hit. This was the point that made the whole get-out-of-bed early bit worth it. The point when she took control of her thoughts and could bury the heartbreak. The moment when she believed she'd actually be able to get through the day and maybe somehow be okay.

Her thighs no longer burned and her head stopped hurting for a few glorious minutes that, when she was lucky, turned into hours. It wasn't exactly peace, but her brain was still. And that was the best she could hope for under the circumstances.

Rounding the next bend, she was in top form. She let go of the belief she was crazy for forcing herself out of bed. She let go of all the thoughts that constantly churned in her head. She just let go.

And then something hit her, knocking her out of her rhythm. A pungent smell blasted her nostrils. At the rate she was breathing, it hit hard. She coughed hard enough to break her stride.

The acrid smell could only come from a dead animal. Out at the lake, that wasn't uncommon. Whatever it was, it must've been dead for days. Gina pulled the collar of her cotton T-shirt up and over to cover her nose and mouth. A few more steps in and her gag reflex engaged.

A side cramp stopped her, doubling her over. She took her earbuds out and glanced around, searching for the cause of the stench. She could make a call to animal control if she could figure out where the smell came from.

Checking underbrush, she heard a sound—like a dog whimpering—to her left. She steeled herself for what she might find and headed toward the noise.

Yesterday's rain had everything soaked. Her running shoes were swamped with mud as she pushed closer to the wounded animal. And then she saw something move under a scrub bush. As she got closer, she saw a black Labrador retriever on his side.

Gina made slow and deliberate movements toward the animal. "You're okay, buddy."

The dog cried as he rolled onto his belly and tried to crawl toward her. She could see his tail wagging. He was friendly. Someone's pet?

Gina had only moved in two days ago. She hadn't had five minutes to introduce herself to the neighbors. Being on acre lots made privacy even easier and that was part of the reason she'd taken over the family cabin. That, and the fact rent was affordable. The restaurant did okay, but there was just enough money to set her mother up with retirement and give Gina enough of a salary to raise her daughter.

"You're a good boy." Gina bent down, making herself as small as possible so the dog wouldn't see her as a threat. He hadn't given her any indication that he would bite. At least not so far. Still, a wounded animal could be unpredictable.

Labradors were great dogs, though, and he seemed to know on instinct she was there to help. He moved again and that's when she saw the blood. A lot of it. Gina moved to his side and smoothed her hand along his body.

And then she found it. Bullet hole. Who in God's name would hurt such a beautiful animal? And how could she live right down the street and not hear it? The storm. Thunder pounded last night. It must've muffled the noise. "Hold on, buddy. We'll get some help." Anger raged through her as she pulled out her cell.

Gina took off the jacket tied around her waist and put pressure on the spot where the animal bled. Her first call was to her mother. The woman had half the town on speed dial. She knew everyone. Gina quickly explained where she was and what she'd found. The second call was to her babysitter to let her know she'd be running late.

The dog stirred. He was trying to get up.

Stroking the animal's fur, tears blinded her. Who could be so cruel?

And then it dawned on her. The acrid smell. It wasn't coming from the animal. She cursed.

He kept trying to get up. Was he trying to take her to his master?

From out of nowhere, Gina heard a twig snap right behind her. She made a move to whirl around. The strike to the back of her head barely registered. Everything went black.

To keep reading Regina's story, click here.

ALSO BY BARB HAN

Don't Mess With Texas Cowboys

Texas Cowboy's Protection

Texas Cowboy Justice

Texas Cowboy's Honor

Texas Cowboy Daddy

Texas Cowboy's Baby

Texas Cowboy's Bride

Texas Cowboy's Family

Texas Cowboy Sheriff

Texas Cowboy Marshal

Texas Cowboy Lawman

Texas Cowboy Officer

Texas Cowboy K9 Patrol

Texas Firebrand

Rancher to the Rescue

Disarming the Rancher

Rancher under Fire

Rancher on the Line

Undercover with the Rancher

Rancher in Danger

Set-Up with the Rancher

Rancher Under the Gun

Taking Cover with the Rancher

Firebrand Cowboys

VAUGHN: Firebrand Cowboys

RAFE: Firebrand Cowboys

MORGAN: Firebrand Cowboys

NICK: Firebrand Cowboys

ROWAN: Firebrand Cowboys

TANNER: Firebrand Cowboys

KEITH: Firebrand Cowboys

TRAVIS: Firebrand Cowboys

KELLAN: Firebrand Cowboys

Cowboys of Cattle Cove

Cowboy Reckoning

Cowboy Cover-up

Cowboy Retribution

Cowboy Judgment

Cowboy Conspiracy

Cowboy Rescue

Cowboy Target

Cowboy Redemption

Cowboy Intrigue

Cowboy Ransom

For more of Barb's books, visit www.BarbHan.com.

ABOUT THE AUTHOR

Barb Han is a USA TODAY and Publisher's Weekly Bestselling Author. Reviewers have called her books "heartfelt" and "exciting."

Barb lives in Texas—her true north—with her adventurous family, a poodle mix, and a spunky rescue who is often referred to as a hot mess. She is the proud owner of too many books (if there is such a thing). When not writing, she can be found exploring new cities, on a mountain either hiking or skiing depending on the season, or swimming in her own backyard.

Sign up for Barb's newsletter at www.BarbHan.com.

GIVEN TO THE GROOM

BY

ANNABELLE WINTERS

Copyright © 2020 by Annabelle Winters
All Rights Reserved by Author
www.annabellewinters.com
ab@annabellewinters.com

If you'd like to copy, reproduce, sell, or distribute any part of this text, please obtain the explicit, written permission of the author first. Note that you should feel free to tell your spouse, lovers, friends, and coworkers how happy this book made you. Have a wonderful evening!

Cover Design by S. Lee

ISBN: 9798618651158

0 1 2 3 4 5 6 7 8 9

1
BELL

Looking back, maybe there were signs.

Like my Uber having *two* drivers, perhaps?

Yup. Two massive, bearded, Mediterranean-looking men dressed in crisp black suits, wearing mirrored Aviator sunglasses, their big heads scanning the surroundings like we were on patrol in a Middle Eastern war-zone or something.

Except we weren't in a Middle Eastern war-zone.

We were in my hometown. A good-sized American city, but not New York or L.A. or Chicago. We're an easy-going bunch here. It's quiet. Peaceful. Even idyllic, like a fairytale or one of those sets in Disneyland's *It's a Small World* ride.

"Um, excuse me," I'd said, leaning forward in my black dress, making sure I covered my cleavage from the two beasts in the front seat. I couldn't see their eyes through the sunglasses, but somehow I sensed they were disciplined enough to not shamelessly stare at my boobs.

Almost like they were *scared* to stare at my boobs.

Like they didn't have the right.

Like my body already belonged to someone else.

"Yes?" one of the men said gruffly but with a strange respect. His voice was heavily accented, and I remember thinking he sounded Greek. I know, because I'm a quarter Greek. My Grandma was a first-generation immigrant from the land of olive oil and ouzo, and she held on to her accent until she died at the ripe old age of ninety-seven. Just last year, actually. Didn't leave me much—though I did pick up her habit of wearing black dresses everywhere.

Even weddings.

"I think there's been a mistake," I'd said to the two men, trying to sound nonchalant, even jovial. "I think maybe you guys picked up the wrong—"

"No mistake," the man says. "We do not make mistakes. No mistake."

Given to the Groom 3

I raised my eyebrows and shook my head. I checked my phone, and when I saw that my real Uber had canceled after waiting for me outside my apartment building, I could feel the fear start to build.

I'm *not* being kidnapped, I'd told myself, smiling in that crazy way people smile in horror movies when they find themselves cornered in a basement and surrounded by zombies or ax-murderers. It's obviously a mistake. Just a mistake.

I'd protested to the men again, but this time they didn't respond. Didn't even turn their oafish heads. I'd looked at my phone again, stared at the "Emergency Call" thingie, and wondered why I wasn't calling 911. After all, they hadn't taken my phone from me.

I'd stared at my phone for what must have been a long time as all kinds of thoughts flowed through my head. Why did I even get into this car? One glance at my Uber app would have told me this wasn't my ride. Oh yeah, and there were two dudes dressed like they're guarding the President sitting inside the black car that I slid my big butt into like I was an airheaded princess. Was I an idiot? Still drunk from last night with the girls?

"It's because it was sunny and calm outside, which lulled me into a false sense of security," I say to myself firmly as I'm forced back to the present, forced to think about what's going on, how I've stepped into what I swear is a different dimension or alternate reality. Yeah, that's probably it. Grandma's probably looking down from the clouds and cackling like she used to in her final years, when she was so far gone in her own world that it was almost sweet. No one knew what she was laughing at then.

Now I know.

She was laughing at my big fat dumb ass.

"So this is what a big fat Greek wedding looks like," I mutter as I feel that manic smile flash on my face again, that crazy-person smile, that smile that's a mixture of dead calm and unbridled panic. Then I look down at myself. Black dress. White flowers. Boobs popping out like they always do because if I wear loose dresses I look like a freakin' beach-ball. I'm big, but I've got a solid hour-glass shape and I don't see a need to hide it.

Though I kinda wanna run and hide now, I think, swallowing hard and frowning as I go over the decisions I made (or *didn't* make . . .) that got me here, to the Grand Hotel downtown, to a wedding that clearly isn't the wedding I'm *supposed* to be attending.

At first I'd thought that maybe this *was* the right wedding. It was a distant acquaintance from highschool. She didn't have many friends back then, and I think she just invited everyone who was still around so she could fill up the room. Free wine and some lobster (or at least shrimp at the buffet . . .)? Sure, I'd thought. Maybe I even meet some guy at the singles table!

"But there aren't any tables, and barely even any guests," I mutter, glancing around the room and noticing that the room's almost deserted. The handful of guests—many of whom look exactly like the goons who drove me here—are just standing on the thick red carpet of the Grand Hotel's ballroom. I don't see a bar. No waiters with trays of champagne and hors d'oeuvres. No buffet table anywhere. Not a shrimp in sight. What kind of a wedding is this? And why am *I* here?

But that's not the real question, is it.

No, the real question isn't really why I'm here.

The question is why am I *still* here?!

I wasn't forced into that car.

Nobody stopped me from calling 911.

Nobody's blocking my exit even now.

So why am I still here?

Why does this feel like it's part of a plan?

Why do I feel like even though it's clearly a mistake, it's also *not* a mistake.

Why do I feel like this is . . .

Like this is . . .

Fate?

Destiny?

Meant-to-be?

My vision narrows to a tunnel, sort of like they say happens when your brain is shutting down and you're about to die or something. But I'm still standing, still calm and panicked at the same time, still asking myself questions that have no logical answers, still wondering if I've lost my mind or if this is all a vivid dream as a result of destroying my brain cells with too much cheap red wine.

"Wake up, Bell," I whisper to myself, wondering if I should reach around and pinch my soft bum. I decide against it, picturing Grandma saying that would be unladylike, that people would think I have a wedgie and am adjusting my panties that keep disappearing between my buttcheeks.

I'm almost hysterical as I blink and sway on my feet. Just a mistake, I tell myself again. No need to create a scene. Just stand quietly at the back of the room and then slip out the door. Hell, you can do it right now. Nobody's looking. And why *would* they look, anyway? I'm just a stranger in the crowd. A random guest at a wedding that most of these guests don't seem particularly excited about. I'm nobody. Invisible. Like a ghost, a fairy, a little pixie! Wheee!

But then suddenly a hush goes over the room and every head turns to me as I stand alone in the back, white flowers in hand, that smile of pure disbelief returning to my face like it's been painted on by the trickster-demon that's pulled me into this alternate dimension, this topsy-turvy world where up is down, left is right, sushi is sashimi, day is night.

A world in which I'm suddenly not invisible, not a no-name guest, not an anonymous flower-girl.

No, I realize as an organ sounds from somewhere in the back . . .

I'm not any of those things.

I'm the . . . the . . .

I'm the bride.

OMFG, I'm the *bride*!

Now the organ plays the tune, and I almost faint on my feet as the sparse crowd parts down the middle, opening up an aisle that leads straight to a raised platform at the far end of the ballroom.

And as I stare at the altar, see the Greek Orthodox priest standing there and smiling like he's in on the joke, I cock my head and wonder . . .

Um, if I'm the bride in this nightmare . . .

Then who's the groom?!

I blink and stare down to the end of the aisle, and I gasp when I see a dark, shadowy figure standing tall like a tower, broad like a bridge, heavy like a wrecking ball.

He's got his back to me, and all I can see is a shock of thick black hair, wild and unruly, long and untamed.

I gasp again as I clutch the flowers, and it's only when I feel myself moving that I realize I've just taken a step towards that beast waiting at the end of the aisle.

Waiting for his bride.

Waiting for me.

2
BRAKOS

How long do I have to wait before this is over and done with, I think as I resist the urge to glance at my diamond-studded Rolex and then up at the Greek Orthodox priest that I suspect has violated all Ten Commandments and then some in his wretched life as holy-man to the most unholy offshoot of the Greek Mafia.

I haven't even bothered to look at my bride-to-be.

Given to the Groom

What fucking difference does it make. This is just an economic alliance, a political necessity, the price I must pay for the life I live. A small price when it's all said and done, of course.

Yes, a small price to pay for a life where I am Master, King, even a god like those who sit on Mount Olympus!

And my life *does* rival those of the Greek Gods of myth, does it not? I live in a palace like Zeus on Olympus, do I not? Bloody hell, I have mansions and palaces all over Europe, in fact. How many mountain-homes does almighty Zeus have? Just one. Besides, a mountain-top is a bloody awful place to live, is it not? The King of Gods has to hang out on the uncomfortable rocks of a cold mountain, freezing his heavenly balls off in robes and sandals while I wear bespoke Italian shoes and tailored French suits, fly in warm luxury and cool comfort between London and Athens on my own thunderbolt of a private jet as I rule my empire with an iron fist.

Of course, it is a small empire. The Greek Mafia is not the fucking *Cosa Nostra*. Hell, the Greek Mafia today isn't even what it used to be—not with the country itself drowning in debt and unemployment. Yes, unemployed young men means recruitment is up. But if legitimate businesses aren't making money in Greece, it trickles down to the illegitimate organizations too.

Which is why I've chosen to expand my horizons. Look overseas.

To America.

And this marriage is the first step in gaining a foothold in the Land of Milk and Honey. We'll get the formalities done and then I'll show her to her separate bedroom. I will not touch her. Will not let her get close to me. Will not make the mistake of letting her believe this is an equal partnership, an equal alliance, a real marriage. I am not her husband but her master, not her partner but her king, not a man but a god. She will understand that from day one.

She will understand that I stand alone.

I rule alone.

And I sleep alone.

That's part of the reason an arranged marriage to a woman I haven't even seen yet is perfect. I'm primed and ready to stay detached forever. Untouchable and invincible forever.

And that shouldn't be hard with this Greek-American mafia princess, I think, taking a long breath as her footfalls on the red carpet draw near. According to the rumors she is not the most attractive pea in the pod. Not that I care. I look down on sex, anyway. To me sex is just a reminder that we evolved from animals and still have to deal with some of the needs of the animal in us. A need that brings lesser men to their knees, makes them bow.

Given to the Groom 11

And Brakos does not bow to the needs of his body.

Brakos does not bow to anything or anyone.

So no, I did not care about what this woman looked like. I had no intention of fucking her anyway. As for perception? Hah! Who gives a damn. I am not some self-conscious socialite mafia prince who gives a shit about being seen at an art opening with some supermodel on my arm. I'm all business. There is nothing in my life but my ambition, my yearning to expand my empire, my craving for power and dominance.

Total power.

Total dominance.

So I'd refused to even look at a photograph of the girl, but some of my guys did, and I'd overheard a couple of them snickering like the *malakus* they are.

"Yah," one of them had said. "Big American girl. Arse bigger than a Santorini sunset."

"Agreed," the other had replied. "Definitely not a supermodel beauty. *Afentikó* must want this alliance very badly to marry a woman who might squash him if she wants to be on top."

I'd stepped out of my chambers after hearing my men insult my unseen bride-to-be, fixing my silencer on my German-engineered Sig Sauer handgun with a casualness that masked the strange way my blood was boiling.

"When I was your age I made comments like that all the time," I'd said with a slow smile as I felt the rage bubble up like a volcano rising to the point of no return. It was a rage I couldn't explain. I am usually cold and composed, my emotions always kept in check. After all, emotions are a man's Achilles Heel. His weakness. His vulnerability. My whole life has been about controlling that weakness—*eliminating* that weakness.

But the anger had taken over as I stared at my two henchmen and gritted my teeth at the way they'd spoken about a woman I hadn't even seen yet, let alone cared about.

"Yes, when I was young I often spoke without thinking first," I'd said to my men, who'd only just noticed the gun hanging loosely in my left hand. "Then I got older and learned the fine art of self-control, of how to shut down your emotions, eliminate that which makes a man weak." Then I'd sighed and shaken my head. "Too bad neither of you will get the chance to grow older."

And as my men cocked their heads in unison like a couple of chickens in the yard, I raised my left hand and put a bullet in each man, right in each fucker's forehead, killing them before the looks of confusion left their smug, greasy faces.

I take a breath now as I think back to that uncharacteristic execution. It's not the killing that bothers me—I've done that so many times it's like brushing my teeth. Nah, it's the fact that I got so uncontrollably angry at those wankers for insulting a woman who is nothing to me. Nothing.

My thoughts trail off as a scent comes to me on the breeze, stiffening me like I'm an animal who's just picked up the musk of his mate. The feeling is so raw it makes my head spin, and I almost stagger on my feet as I blink in confusion. My cock is already hard in my tailored tuxedo trousers, and I know I'm aroused just by that sweet, intoxicating scent coming from the woman walking down the aisle, walking up behind me.

I swallow hard and shake my head. I'm totally disarmed by the way my body is reacting to just her feminine scent. It makes no fucking sense. Humans don't have pheromones like animals do—not according to every scientist out there. Maybe it is perfume?

I sniff the air like a wolf and then shake my shaggy head. No. The aroma that's getting me hard isn't some French perfume—hell, I don't think this woman is wearing any perfume at all.

"I'm not a fucking animal," I growl under my breath, glaring down at my peaked trousers like I'm talking to my stiff cock, ordering it to settle the fuck down like a good boy. "I control my need. I rule myself. I rule my body."

But now those footsteps stop just a few paces behind me, and the blood pounds in my temples as I take deep, gulping breaths like I want to devour the source of that aroma, inhale every last bit of that intoxicating incense, savor every ounce of that seductive scent.

Slowly my head turns like I'm being pulled by a force outside me, like those swarthy Greek gods sitting on Mount Olympus are grinning down at me, like this whole thing was engineered by those wily deities of myth and mischief. After all, the old Greek gods were always depicted as creatures of contrast, contradiction, susceptible to temptations of the flesh. Greek myth is full of stories of gods and half-gods succumbing to the needs of the human, tested by the pull of the flesh.

"Is that what this is, Zeus?" I mutter as I stare at the dark-haired goddess standing beside me. She's dressed in black, dark eye-shadow highlighting her long eyelashes, her thick hourglass shape so pronounced and perfect it feels like she was sculpted by Zeus himself, chiseled out of pure magic, created to tempt me, to test me just like every man who dared call himself a god was tested in the old stories.

Yes, she was created precisely for that purpose, I decide even though I know the thought is fucking insane. But the feeling only gets stronger as I take in the sight of her womanly curves that make my cock throb, her large breasts that make me drool, her wide hips that make me want to drop to my knees, her magnificent bottom that makes me yearn to push my face in there, thick thighs that I want to see spread before me now and forever, from our wedding bed to our death bed.

The feeling only gets stronger, and in a flash of crazed insight I decide that yes, she has indeed been sent by those gods of mischief, to test my arrogant claim that I am one of them.

She has been sent to tempt Brakos.

To test Brakos.

To break Brakos.

A lazy smile breaks on my face as I narrow my green eyes and take another long breath. Her scent invades me like a drug, and I know this is dangerous, that I am being lured like a dumb animal to a trap, drawn in like a bee to honey, facing my downfall in those innocent brown eyes, stumbling towards my doom as I imagine that secret triangle hiding between her thunderous thighs. But I cannot turn away.

If it is a test I must face it. If is a challenge I must conquer it. If it is mine I must seize it, claim it, *own* it!

"Come," I say to her softly but with supreme authority. "Two more steps. Stand beside me, Bellanca."

She blinks as if my voice just snapped her back to reality or something. Only now do I see the odd look in her big brown eyes. It's a strange sort of fear, and as I study her expression I get the sense of turmoil behind those eyes. I get the feeling she's turgid with tension, pregnant with panic, like she doesn't understand why she's here, like maybe she's feeling what I'm feeling, feeling this mysterious pull, like we've been drawn together by fate, by destiny, by forever.

"Bell," she whispers, her full lips barely moving as she stares at me like she's not sure if this is real. "Everyone calls me Bell." Then she blinks and I see the panic almost break through. Almost. "Wait, if this is a mistake, how do you know my name?"

I frown as my temples throb along with my cock. "There is no mistake," I say quietly. "I do not make mistakes. No mistake."

"Um, yeah. That's what those guys said in the car," she says, her voice getting stronger as if she's gaining control of herself, mastering her own emotions, pushing back her panic and facing me in a way nobody's ever faced me. She widens her eyes and puffs her cheeks out and puts on a fake Greek accent that almost makes me laugh. "No mistake," she says in a low voice as she imitates the men I sent to pick her up. "I do not make mistakes," she growls, now clearly imitating me.

"Are you mocking me?" I say, almost puzzled at her boldness. "Do you realize I have killed men for less?"

She snorts and shakes her head like she thinks this is a joke. "OK, now I *know* this is either a prank or a dream. No way you just seriously said that. What are you, some Greek mafia kingpin? Hah! You know, Grandma would have *loved* you! In fact in her final days I remember her going off on some random story about how she was born into the Greek Mafia but had to flee the country as a child after her entire bloodline was wiped out by the Italian Mafia or some shit."

I cock my head and grunt. "Sicilian, actually. The *Cosa Nostra*. But yes. That is correct. Why do you speak of it like it is a joke?"

She stares, a half-smile breaking on her pretty face as her eyes slowly narrow, like she's trying to decide if I am serious. "Um, because that's basically the plotline of the *Godfather Part 2*, buddy. I mean, they were all Italian in the movie, but same lame-ass, overdone plot. Bloodline wiped out in the old country. The child escapes to America. Rises up to reclaim his birthright." She snorts and shakes her head. "Grandma watched those movies a million times. In her final years she pretty much lived in that reality. Talked about how she would have been queen of the Greek mafia or some shit. She was a sweetheart, God bless her. But she also lived in her own head a bit too much. It was all the same to her—fantasy and reality. Like a child. I guess that happens when you get close to the end, face the afterlife, look back on what could have been . . . maybe what you *wish* had been."

I blink again as I wonder what the fuck is going on with this woman. Does she not know who she is?! "Your grandmother's maiden name was Bernice Belitrios, yes?" I say as I think back to the letters and documents I received from Bellanca's grandmother over the past year as we negotiated this arrangement. Letters that were most certainly not written by a senile person. Letters clearly describing events from decades ago, with birth certificates and old court documents from Greece proving her lineage, tracing her bloodline back to the old country, proving beyond a doubt who Bellanca Belitrios is—who she was born to be, whether she knows it or not.

"Blood is destiny, Bellanca. You are who you were born to be," I whisper, my thoughts effortlessly flowing into words almost like I'm losing track of that boundary between the inner world and outside reality. "Always remember that. You are who you were born to be, Bellanca Belitrios."

My vision blurs, and I swear I hear the gods roar with laughter as they see me getting sucked in, getting pulled in, giving in to what feels so real that my whole life up to this point might as well have been a dream.

And before I can stop myself I say the words. The words that bubble up from the depths of my body, the recesses of my soul, the hidden places in my heart.

"And what you were born to be is mine," I whisper as Bellanca moves her lips like a fish out of water, her eyes almost rolling up in her head as if she doesn't believe what's happening, doesn't understand what's happening, can't accept who she is. "You were born to be mine, Bellanca. You *are* mine, Bellanca. You are fucking *mine*!"

She's saying something, but I can't hear shit as that primal need shuts down almost every sense in my body as it takes over, short-circuiting this discussion, sending my entire life careening down a path that could easily lead to my downfall, my destruction, my doom . . .

Or to my destiny.

Then without bothering to hear what she's saying, I turn to the hired priest and snap my fingers. "*Káne miu kínisi*, Father. Skip to the end," I growl from the side of my mouth as I take a step forward, slide my arm around Bellanca's waist, and pull her so hard into me that she gasps and swoons.

And then as the priest babbles out his blessing, I lean in, grab her by the hair, and kiss her. I kiss her hard, with a power and confidence that I know makes the gods gasp as they watch, like they're worried that maybe I just *passed* their fucking test by stepping up and seizing my destiny even though it terrifies me!

"Mine," I say again, breaking from the kiss just long enough to look into her eyes, see our forever somewhere behind her panic and disbelief. "You understand, Bellanca? You're mine. It's done. You're mine."

She's still muttering something as she flails in my arms, and when I finally manage to regain my sense of hearing I realize that she's babbling to herself.

"Wake up, Bell," she's muttering, eyelids fluttering like she thinks this is make-believe, like she's trying to convince herself she's in a dream. "Please wake up, Bell. Wake the fuck *up*!"

3
__BELL__

"**A**h! Thank *God* I'm awake!" I say as relief washes over me when I feel the pillow beneath my head, smell the clean sheets around me, feel the soft mattress beneath me. "Ohmygod, it *was* a dream! Wow. It felt real as hell, didn't it? One of those super-vivid dreams you get where you *know* you're dreaming but you can't wake yourself up, can't even move! Whew. Ugh. Wow. Damn."

I make all sorts of noises that can't be spelled in English, almost cracking myself up, I'm so happy and relieved. Finally I prop myself up against the padded headboard and blink away my brain-fog.

Wait.

Padded headboard?

I don't have a padded headboard.

I have a cheap-ass IKEA bed made of aluminum or some shit.

Oh. My. God.

This isn't my bed . . .

This isn't my bedroom . . .

And this isn't a fucking dream.

I blink, pray, curse, and then blink again, hoping it'll all go away when I open my eyes.

But all I see is a dark, shadowy figure slowly coming into focus.

Tall like a tower. Broad like a bridge. Hair wild and untamed like a beast of pure darkness. Green eyes intense and focused like beams of ethereal light.

Focused on me.

"No," I whisper as the dread rolls through me like waves of that same darkness. "No!"

It's him.

"No," I whisper again, pulling the sheets up to my chin as I stare at this mountain of a man standing at the foot of the bed like a silent guardian at the Gates of Hades. I feel my heart skip four beats and then start pounding so hard I wouldn't be surprised if it jumped out and started doing Zorba's Dance on the sheets, spurting blood everywhere as it giggled and squealed like this is some twisted cartoon.

"No!" I scream, kicking off the sheets and blankets and jumping out of bed, wondering if I should just leap out of the window head-first! They say that if you die in your dream you wake up, right? Unless it's *Nightmare on Elm Street*, of course. "Get away from me!" I scream again, kicking at the heavy comforter which feels like a slab of stone right now.

"Get away from you? I am nowhere near you," he says, smiling as he rubs the thick black stubble on his brutishly square jaw. His olive skin is shining in the golden light of this room, and even as I scream and stumble off the bed in the most unladylike manner possible, for some reason I'm still locked in on his eyes, eyes that are dark green like the ocean during a rainstorm. "And I barely touched you even when I *was* near you."

"Barely?!" I shriek, running to the wall and slamming my palms against it like some hysterical child throwing a tantrum. "That means you *did* touch me!"

The man rubs his jaw again and grins like this is totally fucking amusing to him. I almost laugh out loud at myself when I realize I must look a sight in my crumpled black dress, my hair as wild and untamed as his, my eyes all crusty, face probably all shiny from not exfoliating last night. Oh, and I'm beating my fists against the wall like a deranged child in a mental institution. Maybe I should stop doing that if I want him to stop laughing at me?

He shrugs, his feet firmly rooted in the carpet, his shoulders squared, back straight, eyes focused, everything about him oozing poise and confidence even though I know he's gotta be nuts, right?

"I claimed my bride," he says with a lazy grin. "Are you so far removed from your roots that you find that strange?" Then he loses the grin. "And of course I had to hold you when you fainted in my arms. And then when I carried you up to our hotel suite. And when I put you into bed and—"

"OK, just . . . just *stop*, all right! Just . . . just . . . I mean, who *are* you?" I blurt out, all the words coming at once. I shake my head and look at my hands, wincing when I see a chipped fingernail from clawing at the wallpaper like a psycho.

Then the wince turns to an expression that makes my face hurt when I see a ring on my left hand. A gigantic diamond ring that's so big and shiny I simply blink and straight-up *refuse* to acknowledge its existence. I didn't see that. Nope. Not happening. Somehow I manage to smile when I realize I'm actually really good at denying shit that's shining at me like the freakin' Dog Star. Awesome. Maybe I'll be able to imagine myself out of this madness. Or perhaps argue my way out, at least. "No, seriously. Who are you, and how can you *possibly* be so stupid that you haven't figured out this is a case of mistaken identity?!"

Those green eyes of his flash dark, and I gasp when I see his massive body stiffen. He raises his chin and swallows like he's trying to control himself, hold back his anger.

"Do not call me stupid again, Bellanca," he says softly, with a seriousness that makes my toes curl up. I blink as an image pops into my head . . . an image of him bare-chested like some beast of the jungle, heavy pectorals like slabs of dark marble, arms like tree trunks, palms big and meaty as he growls and advances, muttering something about claiming his bride, maybe *taming* his bride! Ohmygod, I *have* lost my mind!

He's still talking when I manage to push away the vision of him taking me over his shoulder and bounding up the steps of some Greek palace as I shriek and wail and giggle all at once. "And yes, Bellanca. I have indeed figured out this is a case of mistaken identity. Except it is *you* who are mistaken. Mistaken about your *own* identity."

"Oh, right. Because you don't make mistakes," I say, rolling my eyes as I force myself to keep talking. Because if I keep talking, maybe I'll stop thinking. Is it working? Nope. I'm still thinking. Can you think in a dream?

"No, Brakos does not make mistakes. Not even in a dream," he says with that lazy grin. He gestures with his head towards an elegant wooden table near the bed. On it stands a tall glass of some misty liquid. The glass is perfectly placed in the center of the table, on a wooden coaster like it's a setup for a *Home and Lifestyle* photo shoot. "Drink that, Bellanca," he says, his tone effortlessly commanding, like he would have to make an effort to *not* be commanding, if that makes any sense.

"Drink something offered by a random dude in a hotel room? Um, yeah. Sure. Immediately." I roll my eyes and snort, crossing my arms under my boobs and trying to stand as tall as I can, look as elegant and poised as possible—which is kinda hard when you've got crumpled bedsheets wrapped around your ankles and you haven't showered or even brushed your teeth. "You know, I think Brakos *must* be stupid if he thinks I'm gonna just—"

But the sentence ends with a gasp, and before I understand what's happening Brakos has fucking *leapt* across the room and pulled me onto the soft bed, throwing me down with such force I literally bounce three inches off the mattress like it's a trampoline!

And then he's on me, holding me down with his body, pinning my arms above my head as I hyperventilate from the pure shock of how fast he moved, how effortlessly he lifted me off my feet and tossed me onto the bed like I'm a ragdoll! I can tell he's angry, but he's somehow still in control, like he knew *exact-*

ly what he was doing, knew *exactly* where to hold me so I wouldn't get hurt.

I'm still breathing hard as I stare up into Brakos's green eyes. I can feel his hard body pressing against mine, his muscles lining up with my curves almost like we were designed for each other. His masculine musk invades me as I breathe, and I gasp again as I feel myself heat up beneath my black dress, feel my secret wetness ooze from my slit as if my body's totally just surrendering to his dominance, simply opening up for him!

"What are you doing?" I whisper, blinking as I look up at him. He's ruggedly handsome, brutish and swarthy but simultaneously oozing elegance and even royalty. His bone structure looks like it was chiseled from a picture. Strong jawline. High cheekbones. Thick, dark red lips. Damn, our kids will be beautiful, won't they?

Ohmygod, why did I just think that, I wonder in shock as I suddenly become aware of Brakos's erection lined up perfectly with my mound that's now shamelessly wet, straight-up *dripping* through my panties like my slit is wide open, like it's just smiling in glee.

Is my pussy talking to me now? I think as I feel Brakos's body stiffen, see his jaw tighten, those green eyes narrow until he suddenly blinks and looks away like something just occurred to him.

And then he's off me, pulling back with the same smooth, silent grace of an animal. He shakes his head and turns away from me, muttering something in Greek under his breath. As he turns I see the profile of his peaked trousers, and I almost come all over the bed when I see how massively aroused he is.

Aroused for me.

"*Elénxte ton eaftó sas, zóo*," he grunts, finally turning back to me. "Do not worry. I will not hurt you. I will not touch you like . . . like *that*. This is not that sort of marriage, all right?"

"Then what sort of marriage is it?" I say, frowning as I remind myself that by asking that question I'm kinda assuming that we're already . . . married? "Oh, wait. It's *no* sort of marriage, because we're *not* married."

"We were married yesterday, Bellanca," he says without skipping a beat. "Get used to it."

"Um, firstly, this isn't Vegas, buddy. Secondly, I didn't sign a marriage certificate, so even if we *were* in Vegas, having some fake priest mutter some words doesn't mean shit. Not in America, at least."

Brakos steps over to the wooden coffee table and grabs a piece of paper. He holds it up, and I gasp when I see that it's a marriage certificate.

"Right here, Bellanca," he says, holding it to my face and pointing at a signature that's most certainly not mine even though it *is* my name. My full name—Bellanca—which I never use because it sounds like it's from like the 1920s.

"You and I both know I didn't sign that," I say firmly, trying to ignore the strangely warm feeling I get when I see my name right beneath Brakos's elegant signature. Kinda like I was just beneath Brakos himself not so long ago . . .

OK, stop it!

Focus!

"You fainted in my arms when I claimed you. So I signed for you," he says. "Same thing. A husband has the authority to sign for his wife."

"OK, firstly, I don't *faint* like some chick in a romance novel," I snap. "Secondly, who says things like *I claimed you*?! Did I just travel back in time? Am I on a different planet?" I stare at the marriage certificate again and snort. "And finally, even if I ignore the sexism in your belief that a husband has the authority to sign his wife's name on a legal document, it can't apply to the document that actually makes me your wife! That's circular logic! Only an idiot would actually believe—"

I wince and almost bite my tongue off when I see that telltale anger flash in his green eyes. But this time there's also a smile on his thick lips. A smile of triumph. A smile of superiority. A smile of power, dominance, victory.

"Good," he says softly when I realize that I just stopped myself from calling him an idiot without him having to say a damned word! "You are learning, Bellanca."

Now I feel my own anger bubbling up. I'm no pushover, and I realize that with one look he got me to stop talking mid-sentence like I'm some kitten being trained! Dammit!

I almost rattle off a string of insults just to prove that I'm not a pushover, that I don't just bow my head and submit when some egomaniac huffs and puffs and glares and glowers. But I can't do it. I'm actually turned on by his arrogance, even though that's never been something I liked in a guy. Why is that? Why is this over-the-top alpha nonsense getting me hot between my legs, wet beneath my panties, making my nipples stiffen, my toes curl?

I look into his eyes for a long, tense moment, and then I blink and exhale as I suddenly get it, suddenly understand why I'm turned on by an attitude that's always turned me off in the past.

It's because Brakos's arrogance is oddly natural, strangely genuine, not put on or faked. It's not a facade or a front. No pretense. No masquerade. No effort.

This man isn't *trying* to be some alpha beast who needs to control and command . . .

He simply *is* that alpha beast.

And I'm on his bed, wearing his ring, imagining things that just don't make sense, just *can't* make sense. Not in the real world, at least.

I glance towards that piece of paper in his hand

that's totally fake and would be meaningless in a court of law but for some reason feels so damned real right now, so damned meaningful right now.

That strange sense of fantasy washes over me again . . . that weird feeling that made me get into that car yesterday, made me walk down the aisle, made me make choices that no sane woman would ever make. I'm almost in a trance as I look into his eyes, wonder what's going to happen next, what choice I'm going to make next.

And as my mind spins in circles, I watch Brakos step to that table near the bed and reach for that glass. He holds it up, that lazily confident smile still on his face. Then in one smooth motion he brings it to his lips and downs half of it.

"Your turn, Bellanca," he whispers, holding it out for me. I blink at the glass and then into his eyes, cocking my head as I feel a chill go through me. Somehow I know that drinking that simple glass of what's probably just spring water with lemon is deeply meaningful, supremely symbolic. It's like it's an act of trust, an act of partnership, an act of . . . of marriage?

"*This* is my signature on that line, isn't it," I mutter to myself as I slowly rise to my knees on the bed and reach for the glass. It sounds so dramatic and silly, but the feeling is so deep and real I can't deny it. Won't deny it.

My mind swirls like the lemon in the glass as I remember that I still have no real idea what's going on here, that my best guess is still that it's a case of mistaken identity, that for heaven's sakes it *has* to be a mistake. But there's something about how sure Brakos is of himself, so sure of this weird-ass marriage which he says is not "that" kind of marriage—whatever the hell *that* means . . .

Yes, there's something about him that's drawing me in, that's perhaps been drawing me in before I even met him, before I even looked into his green eyes, before I even fainted in his strong arms like some lovesick damsel.

I hold the glass to my lips, the fresh lemon scent drifting through the air like music. I think back to Grandma's final years, the way she'd holed herself up in her home like some weirdo. I loved her like nobody else on earth—shit, I *had* nobody else for most of my childhood: Mom and Dad pretty much worked themselves into early deaths, going sleepless nights and holding down two or three jobs each just to pay the rent and the credit cards. I spent most of those years playing in Grandma's living room while she went on about "the old days" and "what could have been" . . . maybe even what *should* have been . . .

Could it be real, I wonder as I think about how Brakos knew Grandma's name, knew my grandfather's name, knew *my* name. My *Greek* name that not even some of my friends know! How do I explain *that* away? There's something here, isn't there? It might still turn out to be a mistake, of course. It almost certainly *is* a mistake. But . . .

But what if it *isn't* a mistake.

What if it's real?

What if it's . . . forever?

"This is ridiculous," I mutter, shaking my head as I stare through the murky glass. I can see the blurry outline of Brakos through the misty water, like the only way to get clarity is to step into this madness, sign my name on the dotted line, drink the magic elixir this Greek beast just handed me like it's a symbol of my choice, a symbol of my decision, a symbol of . . . of . . .

"A symbol of my madness," I whisper to myself. "That's really what it is. Hah. Maybe the only thing Grandma handed down to me was her freakin' craziness, her ability to live in her own head, live in a fantasy, a world of could-have-been and should-have-been."

But just then I feel a cool breeze around my bare neck, and I shiver. I wonder if a window's open or if the air-conditioning just turned itself on, but the room is silent like a graveyard, almost eerily silent.

I shiver again as I go back over the strange choices I made yesterday—getting into that car, stepping into that ballroom, taking the flowers that someone handed me, and walking down the aisle alone.

Except maybe I didn't walk down the aisle alone,

I think as I feel that cool, otherworldly breeze swirl around me again like it's alive, like it's pure living energy.

Maybe I was being walked down the aisle by the person who'd have given me away if she'd been alive.

Maybe she *did* give me away.

Gave me to the groom.

Gave me to him.

And then I just stop thinking, and with no more hesitation I drink the remaining half of the glass Brakos handed me, feeling the cool lemon-water bring forth a burst of clarity, a feeling of freshness, a sense that I just left the real world behind and stepped into a world of could-have-been and should-have-been . . .

4
<u>BRAKOS</u>

"**T**his should not be happening," I mutter to myself in Greek as I feel a strange breeze in the room, an energy that I swear is alive but invisible, like the gods themselves are intervening in human affairs just like in the old Greek myths. "It has been one day and already I am breaking. Already I am feeling the temptation defeating my will. Already the needs of my body are taking over, rendering me helpless, reminding me that I am an animal and not a man, a creature of flesh and not the god I arrogantly claim to be."

"You sound like Grandma, muttering to yourself in Greek," Bellanca says as she licks her lush lips in a way that makes me yearn to kiss her again, to taste those lips, push my tongue inside her warm mouth. I lick my own lips as I take in the sight of her kneeling on the bed, her wide hips perfectly proportioned for my big body, her magnificent round buttocks designed for my meaty paws. I sniff the air and almost groan out loud when I catch the aroma of her sex, and my knees almost buckle as I imagine pushing my face between those thighs, tearing her wet panties off with my sharp teeth, licking her slit with long, hard strokes, sucking her clit until she screams, fingering her asshole until she comes into my goddamn mouth.

I'd drink from her like her pussy is a magical fountain, I think as I feel myself slipping into a world of fantasy that I swear is more vibrant and vivid than even the highest moments of my "real" life.

Bellanca is saying something, but all the blood has left my head to fill my cock, and all I can think about is her naked like a sunrise, spread like a sacrifice on the altar of our wedding bed. The scent of her sex is so heavy in my nostrils that I have to clench my fists and screw my feet into the carpet just to stop myself from pouncing on her, ripping her clothes to tatters, holding her beautiful body down, pushing my thick

Given to the Groom 37

cock inside her warm cunt and filling her, claiming her, *owning* her . . .

Even if I lose myself in the bargain.

I mutter in Greek again even though I know I must sound like a madman. But my need is overwhelming, my arousal so strong I am even more convinced the gods *are* behind this, that they *have* sent this siren down to earth to show me that I am animal through and through, nothing but a beast destined to roam the earth and satisfy his most basic, most primitive, most primal needs. Because without self-control we are animals, are we not?

Maybe I say to hell with self-control, I wonder as I bite my lip so hard I taste blood in my mouth like it's a brutal reminder that I am a creature of flesh and not divine light. To hell with this obsession to rise beyond the needs of the flesh. After all, every Greek god of the old pantheon fathered a child with a human, did he not?

Of course, each time a god succumbed to the beauty of a human woman it unleashed chaos and destruction, I think as I lick the blood from my lips and take a step towards my temptation, my test, my trial.

Towards my woman.

Towards my wife.

Chaos and destruction, comes the thought again as I unbutton my shirt and rip it off, stretching my arms out wide as Bellanca gasps at the sight of my thick biceps, heavy pectorals, massive shoulders, hard, flat stomach with muscles that look like the foothills of Mount Olympus.

"Brakos, what are you . . ." she whispers, touching her neck and moving back on her knees until she's against the padded headboard of this bed that I don't think is going to hold up to the furious arousal that's rising in me like a volcano building to critical mass, slowly but surely heading for a climax so explosive it will bury the towns and villages in lava and ash, burn down the past and open up a path to the future, to what could be, to what should be.

A path to forever.

"Things have changed, Bellanca," I growl as I unbuckle my heavy leather belt and slide it out. She glances at my peaked black trousers and lets out a soft, silent moan. Her eyes almost roll up in her head, and I swear she just imagined me entering her, invading her, claiming her. I know this is a bloody mistake, but I'm too far gone now. My mind is made up. Hell, my mind has *given* up!

"Um, yeah, things have changed," she stammers, blinking and smiling weakly as she presses her ass against the headboard and places her hands flat by her hips like she's preparing for the onslaught, preparing to be taken, preparing for her . . . husband. "Things have most certainly changed. Yesterday I was planning an evening with free shrimp and cheap wine, and now it's morning and I'm . . . I'm . . ."

Given to the Groom 39

"You are mine," I say firmly, finishing her broken sentence as I step out of my trousers and slowly get on the bed, my weight making the mattress bend, the bedframe creak. "Now it is morning and you are mine, Bellanca. My wife. My woman. My forever."

"Brakos, listen," she mutters, brushing a strand of her brown hair from her forehead as I move towards her, my massive fists clenching and releasing, my cock almost ripping through my black silk underwear that's glistening with the pre-cum that's already soaked through. "Listen, Brakos. I still think there's been a mistake. I'm not who you think I am."

"And I am not who I thought I was, Bellanca," I growl as I finally get to her and run my hands down along her sides as I take in the sight of her heavy cleavage, inhale her scent, kiss her forehead gently just to get a taste of her sweetness. "I thought I was a god, but you reminded me I am still an animal. I thought I was destined to rule alone, but you make me want to bow down, to kneel, to give you everything. I thought this marriage was a transaction, an economic alliance, just business, fake like plastic flowers or artificial sweetener. But instead it feels more real than anything in my life, Bellanca. The work of the gods. The machinations of the angels and the demons working together." I'm babbling like a bloody idiot, but I believe every word that comes from my bleeding lips. I slide my hands down her thighs and then up her dress, groaning as her lustrous ass fills my big palms. I yank her panties up until they're deep in her asscrack, pressing my erection against her wet crotch and holding myself there as I lean in and gently kiss her lips even though my body is straining to take her hard and deep, with fury and force, with all the animal and the god in me. With all the man in me.

"You sound as crazy as I must be to still be here," she murmurs. "Plastic flowers? Artificial sweetener? Who talks like that?"

I grunt as I kiss her again. Fuck, she tastes like sugar. She smells like flowers. "You know," I say with a grin as I bring my hands out from beneath her dress and stroke her lips, caress her smooth round cheeks. "We have not even been married a day and already you have called me stupid, idiotic, and now crazy." I snort and glance off to the side for a moment. "*Gamó*, Bellanca. Last week I executed two men simply because they—"

"Wait, what? You . . . you *executed* someone?! What do you mean you *executed* someone?" she says.

"Did I not speak clearly enough, Bellanca?" I say. "I may have a thick Greek accent, but I spend half my time in London and my English is impeccable."

She blinks and tries to move her head, but she can't because of the way I'm cupping her face in my big palms. "It's not your English," she says. "It's . . . I mean, you're just messing with me, aren't you?"

"If by messing you mean am I joking, then let

me be clear, Bellanca: I am *not* messing with you. I am *not* making a joke. What am I, a clown?" I say through gritted teeth. "Who do you think I am, Bellanca? Who do you think *we* are?"

"I don't *know* who you are, Brakos!" she says, and I see a hint of panic in her big brown eyes, like the fear she's been closing herself from is pushing its way back into her, pulling her away from me.

I take a slow breath as I remind myself that best I can tell, this woman does not know the meaning of heritage, the responsibility of a bloodline. She does not understand that blood and destiny are the same thing. "Do not pretend, Bellanca," I say as I smell her hair, feel my cock pressing against her mound in a way that almost makes me explode. "I know your grandmother passed away before she could see the wedding through, but surely she told you what was happening, what this is, who I am, who *you* are."

"Um, my grandmother spent most of her final years in her freakin' attic, babbling away in Greek, all right?" she snaps at me, an incredulous expression on her pretty face. I see a flash of innocence in those eyes, and I bite my lip again. "I mean, she wasn't senile or anything. But she just kinda lived in her own head, in her own world, always talking about the past, the old country."

"And you were not paying attention," I say, shaking my head. "You bloody Americans. Self-centered.

Insular. Closed off from the rest of the world. Closed off from where you all came from."

"Um, that's the *point* of America, you Greek dinosaur," she says, and now I see the fire in those eyes that were just wide with fear and innocence. "When you come to America, it doesn't *matter* where you came from, who you were in the old country. You can be *anyone* in America. You're not bound by bloodlines and ancestors and whatnot. You *choose* who you want to be. That's the idea. That's the point of freedom, of democracy."

I snort and shake my head. "Do not lecture me on democracy, Bellanca. The Greeks *invented* democracy." I shake my head again. "All right. I understand that your generation has no patience for the stories of their grandparents. But the letters and documents I got from Bernice Belitrios were perfectly preserved, beautifully organized. It was not the work of some senile old woman."

"I told you, Grandma wasn't *senile*," Bellanca says. "She was just . . . just *weird*. She watched movies all day and all night." She sighs and shakes her head. "Mostly gangster movies. Actually, *only* gangster movies." Then she blinks and frowns. "I mean, yeah, there was this one recent outburst where she insisted she was a mafia princess and her family had been wiped out in Athens so she fled to America. But it was just one time, and so I just laughed it off because she'd been awake for like three days watching

Given to the Groom

the entire *Godfather* series while smoking filterless cigarettes and drinking Greek wine."

I stare at her as now I wonder if *she* is messing with *me*. "You . . . you *laughed* it off? You cannot be serious! Your grandmother tries to tell you about your heritage, your bloodline, your ancestry, and you laugh it off?"

"Well, when you spend all your time alone, immersed in some fictional world, it's easy to lose track of what's real and what isn't," Bellanca says, blinking again as I see the first shadow of doubt in her eyes. "And it's not like she'd been talking about it for years or anything. It was just last year that she went off the deep end about the old country and what should have been and could have been and whatever. I mean, my parents never said anything about it before *they* died, either. And like I said, Grandma only *started* talking about it last year. She was already pretty old, Brakos. Already fading."

Bellanca's voice goes soft, and I loosen my hold on her cheeks, caressing her smooth skin gently with the back of my fingers. I try to put things together—which is damned hard when most of the blood has abandoned my brain for my balls.

"Brakos, if all this were true, why would Grandma kept quiet about it for so many years?" Bellanca continues, her voice trembling as if she's starting to second-guess herself, second-guess everything.

I grit my teeth as I think back to what I know about

the history of the Greek mafia. The Belitrios Family was strong, brutal but fair, offering protection to those who needed it, justice for those who paid for it. But their downfall was sudden, was it not? The records are sketchy—after all, all of this occurred well before everyone and his pet Chihuahua had their own Instagram live-stream or whatever bullshit the kids do these days with their phones.

"Fear," I say absentmindedly. "Denial. A need to bury the past and start a new life in America, just like you said." Now the pieces begin to come together—not all the pieces, but enough that I slowly nod my head and narrow my eyes as I stroke Bellanca's cheek. "Her parents and siblings were killed, Bellanca. She must have barely escaped with her own life. She was just a girl when she fled. Of course she wanted to have nothing to do with that world, with that life. Maybe at some point she even stopped believing it was real, like it was just a dream—probably a nightmare, actually."

"So what happened suddenly at the end of her life to change her mind?" Bellanca says, her voice peaked with disbelief, but the kind of disbelief that happens when you know that what seems insane might be the truth. "She got wasted, binge-watched some gangster movies, thought about the old days and decided hey, let's set my grand-daughter up with some Greek mafia kingpin so she can live the life that was taken from me? You think that's a reasonable fucking explanation for what's happening here?!"

I take a breath and grunt as I stroke her soft hair. "I will admit it is a bit far-fetched, but the few facts we have fit the explanation," I say with a cool confidence that's oozing through me as I feel things fit tighter together even though I do not have all the facts, will perhaps never have all the facts.

But perhaps I do not need all the facts, I think as I glance down at the ring I placed on her finger, a diamond that reminds me that I still have a chance to pass this test, that a god creates his own world, bends reality to fit his needs. Facts? To hell with facts.

"Facts do not matter as much as we think," I whisper as my thoughts and speech blend together seamlessly like fiction and reality are joining in a surreal dance that makes my head spin, makes my heart pound, makes me tighten my grip on Bellanca even as I feel my grip on the real world slip away. "No, facts do not matter. Not when it feels like this, Bellanca. Not when it feels like this."

"It's . . . it's Bell," she whispers up at me as I firmly fist her hair with one hand and cup her ass with the other until she's completely under my control. "My name's Bell. Everyone calls me Bell."

Slowly I shake my head as I lean in and lick her lips with the tip of my tongue. "Not anymore," I growl. "You are Bellanca. Bellanca, wife of Brakos. And one more thing, Bellanca, wife of Brakos: This was not a setup, not a hookup, not an arranged meeting. You were given to me, Bellanca. Simple as that. You were *given* to me, and you are mine. Mine, you hear. All mine."

She tries to say something, but I am done talking. The facts can wait. The details can wait. Fucking *everything* can wait.

Because there's something that needs to happen now.

Right now.

So with the gods of old watching from their theater seats on the misty slopes of Mount Olympus, I give in to the siren song of my curvy bride, say to hell with what I thought I was, to hell with the facts, the details, the what or when or why or how.

All that matters is now.

All that counts is here.

Because here, in my arms, is my forever.

5
__BELL__

Bellanca.
Wife of Brakos.
You are Bellanca now.
Bellanca always.
Bellanca forever.

His voice echoes in my head even as his tongue drives into my mouth, even as his fingers claw at my hair, one hand cups my ass as he grinds into me, kissing me with a need so furious, an energy so dominant, so possessive, so all-encompassing that I can barely see straight.

I am Bellanca now, I say to myself as I finally bring my arms up and embrace my husband, a man whose name I didn't know until after our wedding. A man I still don't know but am giving myself to like it's the most natural thing in the world. Was this what it was like a hundred years ago, in the old country, the old world, a world where men took what they wanted and women gasped and mewled and whimpered in submission? Am I weak for submitting? Am I a pushover for breaking? *Did* I break?

Or did I break him . . .

The thought hits me like a hammer just as Brakos snaps the waistband of my panties with one hand, his strong fingers breaking the elastic with such ease I can't help but wonder what he could do to a man's neck if he chose to use his full strength. The thought somehow gets my arousal to spike upwards, and before I know it I'm hungrily kissing him back as he rubs my mound hard and rough from beneath, fingering my cunt so deep my wetness pours out like a river.

"I told myself I would not touch you," he growls against my cheek as he drives three fingers into my vagina and curls them up against the sensitive front wall. "And now all I can think about is touching you, taking you, possessing you, owning you. I lasted less than a day with you, Bellanca. You broke me after one day of marriage. Only the gods know what will become of me after thirty years of marriage."

"I don't think I'm gonna last thirty years if this is how . . ." I start to say, but I can't finish the sentence because in a swift, violent movement Brakos yanks me down from my kneeling position, slams me flat on the bed with a force that takes my breath away, spreads my thighs so wide it hurts, and then rams his face into my wide-open slit with a roar that I swear sounds like some beast of myth is between my legs.

I scream as I come all over his face, all over my thighs, soaking the sheets as Brakos devours my pussy like a man gone mad. Then I come again as he slides one hand up along my thrashing body, pushing my dress up, snapping my bra's underwire like it's a twig, pinching my nipples with brutish urgency and gripping my throat in a way that sends a wild mix of fear and arousal ripping through me.

Brakos drives his tongue in and out of me with such speed and urgency that I don't know if I'm coming again or just never stopped coming. It's like he's lost control, but at the same time the way he's gripping my throat with a mixture of tenderness and dominance is messing with my head. The pressure is almost perfect—just enough for me to know I'm under his control but not enough to hurt me. Just enough for the fear to take me to a place I didn't know I wanted to go, but not enough to take me to a point where I'm actually scared for my life.

I buck my hips and come once more for Brakos,

arching my neck back and licking my lips in ecstasy as I feel him slide his other hand beneath my raised rump and push his thick middle finger into my asshole. The sensation is sublime, and I moan as my consciousness tries to come to terms with how totally Brakos is taking me. His tongue deep in my vagina, one finger curled inside my ass, his strong right hand gripping my throat as I come like a woman possessed.

And then suddenly he's gone, releasing me from his grip and pulling out of me from everywhere at once. I flick my eyes open as I wonder again that maybe it *was* all a dream, and I almost cry out, almost reach out to pull myself back into the dream that I so desperately wanted to escape just a few minutes ago!

I'm thrashing on the bed as I try to focus, and when I manage to see straight I almost go blind with arousal.

Brakos has drawn back and torn his silk underwear off his muscular hips like he's a freakin' werewolf going insane under a full moon, and I stare as his cock springs out, fully hard, massively erect, the sudden release spraying pre-cum all over my stomach and breasts like he's marking me. All I can do is stare at his monstrous shaft that I swear looks thicker than a tree-trunk. His cockhead shines like a dark red comet, oozing his clean natural oil, and all I can think about is how deep he's going to push that thing, how hard he's going to drive it in, how full I'm going to be when he empties those big Greek balls inside me.

"Ohmygod, what's happening to me?" I mutter as I watch Brakos grasp his cock and slap it against my clit until I'm convulsing in ecstasy. The thoughts ripping through me are so vulgar, so twisted, so primal I seriously wonder if I've lost my mind.

But then Brakos looks me in the eye and smiles, and as I feel his cockhead spread the mouth of my slit, feel his shaft open me up like I've never been opened, feel his length go deeper than I thought was possible, I *know* I've lost my damned mind.

"The gods brought us together," Brakos groans as he finally enters me all the way and holds himself there, his cock so impossibly deep that I feel it in my throat. "And when I am finished not even the gods will be able to tear us apart."

6
__BRAKOS__

My own world is torn apart as I enter Bellanca with all the man in me, all the man I am, all the *everything* I am. In fact it does not matter what I am anymore, what I thought I was, what I yearned to be.

A god? An animal? King? Boss?

None of those labels means a thing when I'm faced with the terrible truth:

All I am is hers.

That is all.

My eyes roll up in my head and I roar to the heavens as her warmth overwhelms me, her soft sex opens for me, opens for Brakos, opens for her husband.

I drive into her and hold myself there, look into her big brown eyes that are misty and unfocused but yet looking right into me. I caress her hair as I feel her tight, warm vagina press against my cock like she's holding me in there.

"You are so warm, Bellanca," I whisper, flexing inside her and making her seize up. I am so damned deep I know I'm reaching places that are untouched inside her, claiming a part of her that no man has ever claimed, no man *could* ever claim. "So bloody tight, Bellanca."

"Bellanca . . ." she whispers as I start to move inside her. "It's so strange to hear someone call me that. It sounds so new, but still old in a way. Bellanca."

"That is what this feels like, yes?" I say softly even as I move harder inside her, the fire of my need burning brighter, my cock flexing on its own as I pull back and then push deep once more. "New, but still old. Our first time even though it feels like forever."

"Plastic flowers and artificial sweetener," she mutters through a trembling smile as I lick her neck, suck her boobs, slide my hands beneath her rump and raise her ass as the animal in me starts to come alive, like it's been waiting to be taken off the leash.

"I come from a long line of epic Greek poets, clearly," I growl, biting down gently on her left nipple and making her gasp. "And our children will inherit my way with verse."

"Your vay with werse?" she says, giggling and then groaning as I dig my fingers into her buttocks and raise her hips so I can drag my cockhead against the front wall of her vagina as I fuck her. "Oh, shit. Do that, Brakos. Oh, God, keep doing that. Oh. Oh. *Oh*!"

She comes all over my balls as I hit her fibrous g-spot and flex my cock to apply just the right amount of pressure. Then I reach between us and rub her clit with my thumb, licking my lips and grinning when I feel her body thrash and flail beneath me as I take her climax over the top, watch her orgasm rise like a serpent from the sea and then crash down like a tidal wave hitting the shore.

And now my own need to take her rises up like a monster of the underworld, and as Bellanca comes in my arms I plunge myself deep into her dark valley, bringing forth a scream that I know comes from the deepest part of her soul, the part that now belongs to me.

I slam my powerful hips against hers, driving my cock in so hard my balls slap against her skin. And now I'm pounding, plundering, taking everything, claiming it all. I grab her by the back of the neck, one hand still firmly gripping her ass as I furiously

Given to the Groom 55

take her. She's hunched over, mouth hanging open in shock as she stares down between us at the sight of my mammoth cock spreading her slit so wide I know she's never been opened up like this.

Her soft pubic curls are glistening with our juices, the drops of our natural oils shining like diamonds. I look into her eyes and then we both look down along our naked bodies like we're seeing ourselves for the first time.

"You're so damned beautiful, Bellanca," I mutter as I see her magnificent breasts shudder in the most exhilarating way each time I slam my cock back into her. "Your body was built for mine. Built for our children."

I see her face go flush, her eyelids fluttering like she's panicking at the reminder of the reality that's unfolding here. The reality that Brakos is going to empty his balls into her, fill her with his seed, take her the way a man is supposed to take a woman.

"You hear me, Bellanca?" I growl, gritting my teeth as I feel my climax start to build from the depths of my heavy balls. "You feel me? You feel this? You feel . . . *us*?"

She nods her head and moves her lips, and I look into her eyes and just *explode*, my climax coming so hard and strong that I almost black out. It has been years since I allowed myself to touch a woman, but even in my wildest days I know it never felt like this. This is special. This is real. This is . . .

"*Se agapo!*" I roar as my seed erupts inside her, my semen shooting against the farthest reaches of her cunt, flooding her so fast she's overflowing down my shaft even as I pump more into her. My balls clench and release, delivering load after load into my wife as if I've been saving it all for her. "*Se agapo!*"

The blood pounds in my head as I pull back and drive into her again, my orgasm still going, my hard body clenching along with my balls. My fingers are digging so hard into Bellanca's ass I know they will leave marks on her smooth skin. I'm pounding her so deep I know she will be stiff in the morning. She's screaming and wailing, thrashing and flailing. But she's got her arms around me, and as I feel her nails draw blood from my back, ripping through flesh and skin, I roar and lick my lips, welcoming the pain, reveling in it, taking in the smell of blood and sex, inhaling the aroma of our union.

With one last massive push I finish inside Bellanca, emptying myself into her in ways that seem to go beyond the physical, like I have given much more than just my seed, that she has accepted much more than just my sex.

And finally I collapse on her, my weight pressing her body into the mattress and pushing her so deep I wonder if I'm smothering her.

But then I feel her fingers in my thick black hair, and I smile and kiss her neck.

"*Saga-po?*" she says from beneath me, her voice muffled. "What does that mean?"

I grunt and slowly pull back, frowning as I look upon her face that's streaked from the strain, peaked from the passion. "Are you bloody serious? What kind of a Greek are you?"

"The American kind," she says. "Are you gonna answer me or do I have to push you off me and check the internet?"

"Good luck pushing me off you," I say, spreading my arms out wide and grinning as she gasps from the enormity of my weight.

"I'm surprisingly strong, actually," she says, grunting as she tries to push me off her. She is in fact quite strong, but her efforts cannot work. "Oof. Well, maybe not *that* strong. What do you eat? Concrete?"

I laugh and slowly roll off her, groaning in satisfaction as my cock slides out from her pussy, a long trail of my thick semen still connecting us as I grope for the side-table. "Speaking of food, you have not eaten," I say, reaching for the room-service menu and opening it up as I draw Bellanca into my body. She cuddles against me, and I can barely read the menu as a feeling of warmth flows through me like a magic spell.

"*Se agapo*," I say, caressing her soft hair as I watch her read the menu like she's only just realizing that she must not have eaten in maybe twenty-four hours! "You really do not know what that means?"

"I told you, we speak American here, not Greek," she says firmly, reaching out and flipping the page. "Are you gonna tell me or do I have to guess?"

I turn her head so she's forced to look into my eyes. "Guess," I say. "Look into my eyes and you will know what it means."

Bellanca looks into my eyes. She's smiling at first, but then I can see the understanding wash over her and I know she feels it, feels this warmth that's bonding us together, cementing our union, guaranteeing our forever.

"Do you understand what it means now, Bellanca?" I whisper.

She blinks and then nods, and I lean in and kiss her with a gentleness that I didn't think I had in me.

"Yes," I say as she nuzzles against me like a kitten. "That is exactly what it means. It means I love you. I love you, Bellanca. I love you."

7
__BELL__

I love you.

The words echo in my head as I pretend to read the room-service menu. Of course, I can't read shit. The letters are dancing on the page like they're alive, swirling around and switching places to form new words that make me giggle.

I'm nestled into Brakos's big body, and I smile as his earthy scent comes to me, his musk filling me in a way that makes me think I don't need to eat. All I need is right here. All I need is this.

All I need is him.

"Brakos," I whisper, blinking as I look up past his thick, sinewy neck, up at his chiseled face, into those green eyes that say so much even though I know they're hiding so much more. Hiding things a part of me doesn't *want* to know! "Brakos, I . . . I . . ."

"You do not need to say it," he says with a grunt. "I know it. Your body has told me what I need to know. When your American brain catches up, you can say it then." He grabs the menu from me and flips through the pages, his face darkening as I stare at him, wondering if he's really just decided that I . . . that I love him!

Do I love him?

But I can't be in love so soon!

But how can I *not* be in love when it feels like this?

I look up at him again, about to say what I know feels right even though it's logically impossible, even though it makes no sense, even though--

But once again Brakos stops me with just his eyes. One slow blink is all it takes, and I just melt when I understand that he doesn't need to hear me say it, doesn't need to put me through the mental anguish of fighting my modern-ass sensibilities. He's too self-confident and old-fashioned for that.

No, he doesn't need me to say it.

Given to the Groom

He knows it.

I know it.

And with one more slow, knowing blink, Brakos turns back to the menu and it's done.

We're in love.

We're married.

So what now?

"Now, we feast. Brakos is hungry, even if you are not," he says, and the mood suddenly lightens like we just walked out of the wedding chapel into a shower of rose petals and rice! I'm almost delirious with this feeling, this sudden certainty, this overwhelming peace, and I just lean my head back and laugh.

"What's with referring to yourself in the third person?" I finally say as he reaches out a muscled arm and paws at the hotel phone. "You know nobody does that in real life, right?"

"Then perhaps this is not real life," he quips, his frown cutting deeper as he gets to the last page of the menu and then tosses it across the room. He's on the phone now, and I watch in some combination of disbelief and amusement. "Hello? Yes. This is Brakos. What selection of caviars do you have in the hotel?" His thick black eyebrows move like snakes as I hear a hesitant reply from Room Service. "That is unacceptable! You call yourself the Grand Hotel? How can you say you are grand when you do not offer Beluga Caviar! Preposterous! Connect me to the CEO immediately, please. No, not the bloody hotel manager. I want to speak to the person who runs the company. This has already escalated beyond the scope of your little hotel manager. It is now a global issue, and Brakos will solve it for you so you can at least *pretend* to be a real hotel. Yes, I will hold. But hurry up or else Brakos will come down there himself, and trust me, you do not want Brakos in your bloody kitchen."

I giggle and shake my head as I imagine the poor Room Service operator scrambling for someone to take over so he won't have to deal with some madman who refers to himself in the third person.

"Um, you know this isn't New York or London or Paris, right?" I say. "The Grand Hotel is pretty much the best this town has to offer. And I'd bet you're the first person in twenty years to ask about their selection of freakin' *caviars*!" I take a breath as I see Brakos's heavy chest move up and down as he stays on hold. "Maybe they have some sushi. California rolls are fun!"

"Fake crabmeat and rubbery cucumber? I would rather eat the fucking carpet," he grunts, glaring at the phone and then tossing it across the room in generally the same direction as the room-service menu. "This is not a town. It is a bloody *village*. Why in Zeus's name did Bernice Belitrios choose this place as headquarters of her empire?"

I stare at Brakos, wondering if he's still kidding. "Um, Bernice's *what*?"

Given to the Groom 63

"Empire," Brakos grunts, clenching his jaw and looking up at the ceiling like he's still thinking about how to get some Beluga Caviar for his refined palate. "Her operation. Her organization. The shell companies she used to launder the money. The network of underground businesses ranging from gambling to protection to hired hits to—"

I burst into laughter, smacking Brakos on the chest. "Oh, my God! You *totally* had me going there. Hired hits? Grandma? That's awesome. And the dead-pan delivery? Solid. Well done. And all this while I thought Brakos was a stone cold killer without a funny-bone in his body."

But Brakos doesn't laugh, and when I see the way he's looking at me, I stop laughing too.

"What?" I say. "Don't tell me you're pissed that I implied you *aren't* a bad-ass killer mafia guy. I'm sure you're very good at killing people."

I try to smile, but I can't get myself to do it because a chill is running through my body, chasing away that wonderful warmth I felt just a moment ago. And then suddenly all those thoughts that I'd somehow pushed away come rushing back like a dam has broken, and I feel light-headed when I remember what got us here . . . what got *Brakos* here.

"OK, maybe I do need to eat something," I say. "I'm not thinking clearly."

Brakos slowly raises his head and looks for the phone, which is all the way across the room and in fact might be broken. "Yes, I will order food," he says, frowning in a way that I can tell means the wheels are turning in his head too. What's he thinking? Is he doubting the reality of what's happening too? Shit, what *is* the reality of what's happening?! What did Grandma tell this guy to drag his ass all the way from Greece to this town, to this moment, to . . . to me?!

I watch as Brakos smoothly rises up off the bed, and I blink at the sight of his muscled body from behind. He kinda does look like a Greek god, it occurs to me as I cross my legs and stare at his glistening haunches as he stands naked in the sunlight streaming through the crack in the curtain.

Somehow the phone still works, and he barks some orders into it and tosses it back down to the carpet. Then he turns to me and stands tall and broad, not a shred of self-consciousness as he faces me in all his naked glory.

"Along with proof of her ancestry, Bernice Belitrios sent me a detailed outline of her operations in the United States," he says.

"Operations?! Brakos, Grandma barely left her home! Barely left her spot in front of the freakin' TV? Trust me, she was *not* running some nationwide criminal enterprise! I mean, you said it yourself: If she was some secret gangster-bitch, why the hell would she choose a no-name town like this for her headquarters?"

"Precisely *because* it is a no-name town in Middle America," Brakos says, crossing his arms over his chest and looking down at me like I'm a schoolgirl. "I run my own organization from a small town a hundred miles away from Athens. Our business is all about keeping a low profile. Flying under the radar. That's why all the shell businesses, the need to launder money through legitimate businesses. Remember, Al Capone was finally brought down not by the FBI but by the IRS."

I rub my eyes and shake my head. I don't even know where to start. I don't know if I'm the fool or if he's the fool or if Grandma's somehow managed to make fools of everyone—maybe even *herself*! Hell, maybe she *was* senile in some strange way that expressed itself like this. Maybe she created this world in her own head and then produced all kinds of documents and whatnot in some obsession to make it real.

Or maybe . . .

Maybe it *is* real.

And I just hug myself and curl up into a ball on the big, empty bed, not sure if I want to laugh or cry or just scream. I mean, there's no way in hell Grandma was running some mafia empire from her freakin' attic! But at the same time, clearly she managed to convince Brakos she was doing *exactly* that! So what's the truth? I mean, Grandma was smart as hell, a determined, strong-ass woman. She saw her parents and siblings murdered, according to Brakos. She got on a freakin' ship and sailed her teenage butt across the world and started a life in America. She married, lost her husband early, supported her family, and then even supported me after Mom and Dad died! Shit, maybe she *was* what Brakos thinks she was! I mean, there are all sorts of unbelievable stories of people living double lives, secret lives. What if it *is* true?

And then suddenly the *opposite* fear rips through me as I see a shadow pass across Brakos's dark face. The face of the man who just took me as his. The face of the man I just gave myself to, the man *Grandma* gave me to!

Yes, suddenly I'm scared of the exact opposite . . .

What if Grandma *did* make it all up?

What if she *did* somehow manage to trick Brakos into thinking she was running some secret Greek Mafia empire in America, that I was the heir to some underground throne that would be handed over to him in this arranged marriage?!

And if she *did* make it all up, what happens when Brakos figures that out?!

What happens to the "wedding" that happened just a day ago?

What happens to what just happened between us?

What happens to us?

I feel that light-headedness return with such force I almost throw up. I'm looking right into Brakos's

Given to the Groom 67

devilishly green eyes, and I know—I just *know*—he's thinking the same thing! Ohmygod, what next? What do I do? What if this *is* a mistake, but a totally different sort of mistake than I thought it was!

I blink three times as I try to think my way through this. There are so many unanswered questions—so many questions that are probably unanswerable since Grandma's dead. But the one that's really bothering me is why . . .

Why didn't she tell me?

If she'd taken this to the point where she'd arranged a fucking wedding for me, why the hell wouldn't she *tell* me?! That just doesn't fit!

There's a knock at the door, and I'm startled out of my thoughts as I frantically grab my dress and pull it on. Brakos makes no move, but then I can see he realizes it must be Room Service, and he sighs and heads toward the bathroom.

"You can let them in when you're dressed," he says. "My wallet is on the table for a tip."

I watch as Brakos slams the bathroom door shut, and then I'm alone. Absentmindedly I reach for his wallet, my eyes going wide when I see that it's stacked with hundreds. *Hundreds* of hundreds, it seems.

My vision goes blurry as the stacked wallet reminds me that Brakos didn't want this marriage for money.

He wanted it for power.

I hear it in the words he uses . . .

Empire.

Kingdom.

Conquest.

I hear it in the way he talks about himself in third person like he is somehow larger than his own life, more than just a man . . .

And how can I give him that kind of power?! What does he want from me?! From this marriage?!

"I can't," I stammer, straightening my hastily pulled-on dress and grabbing my stuff, stepping into my shoes, reaching for the door and managing to pull it open just in time so I don't hit my own freakin' face on it. "I just . . . *can't!*"

Somehow I stuff a couple of hundreds in the bewildered waiter's hand, and then I'm running down the carpeted hallways, tears streaming down my face, tears of pure confusion, pure panic, pure madness.

I stumble out the side door, squinting in the sunlight as I take gulping breaths of fresh air. I wish I could convince myself I was still dreaming, but this is fucking real. Real and terrifying.

Terrifying because at the bottom of the confusion and panic I feel something rock steady, a part of me that's completely calm, supremely stable, perfectly poised. It's almost like there's a part of me that's just watching in amusement as I thrash about trying to make sense of the facts, put the pieces together, solve the puzzle just so my brain doesn't explode.

And as I hail a taxi and slide into the backseat, I glance at my finger and see that diamond staring back at me with the same certainty I feel deep inside my soul. And I remember what Brakos said to me when he decided to take me as his, to claim me as his woman, his wife, his forever:

"To hell with the facts," he'd growled in his thick accent. "The facts do not matter, Bellanca. Not when it feels like this."

"Not when it feels like this," I whisper, touching that ring and exhaling slowly. "Not when it feels like this."

8
BELL

"It feels like no one's been in here since she died," I say out loud as I step through the front door of Grandma's house.

Well, my house now, I suppose. Grandma left it to me in her will. It's not worth much—real estate prices in this town aren't that hot, and this isn't a great part of town. Part of me wants to hold onto it, maybe live here. But it's not in great shape, and I'd have

Given to the Groom

to put a lot of money into getting things fixed up. I knew it made sense to clean it out and then sell. I needed the money anyway, and I was happy in my little one-bedroom apartment.

"Well, of course no one's been in here," I say, once again talking out loud like I'm hoping it'll scare the ghosts away. I pop open a couple of windows to air out the place, and then I take a breath and look around.

It looks the way it did after I cleaned up following the small post-funeral reception. I haven't been back here since then—mostly because I was busy, but also because I didn't want to deal with cleaning all the crap out of the basement and attic. Maybe I was afraid of what I'd find in there?

But now I'm not afraid. Now I'm praying I'll find something—anything—that brings me some peace, some clarity, maybe even closure. Was Grandma who Brakos thinks she is? Am I who Brakos thinks I am?

And maybe at the end of it I'll know if *we* are what I think we are.

Before I know it I'm in the attic, which is where Grandma spent most of her final months, it seemed. I wasn't around that much. I was busy, yeah, but that wasn't the only reason, it occurs to me as I think back. There were times I'd call and say I'd come over and we could order food and watch a movie. But then she'd decline, saying stuff like she was tired or whatever. I wasn't too worried—after all, the woman seemed healthy until that sudden heart attack. Of course, that made it all the more shocking when she died, but Grandma had always said she wanted to go quickly.

"If I end up in a hospital bed, pissing in a bag, I want you to put a bullet right here," she'd said to me once, tapping her forehead and looking at me with unflinching seriousness. "Two bullets, actually. Just to make sure. You never know. They say the spirit lingers around for a while if there's unfinished business."

"Um, and finishing you off with an execution-style double-tap in Our Lord of Eternal Mercy Hospital is gonna take care of *what* unfinished business, exactly?" I'd said, snorting at Grandma's humor, which could sometimes get weirdly dark.

"That's *my* business, not yours," she'd told me. "You just go about your life. Don't worry about me. How's that boyfriend, by the way?" she'd added with a gleam in her eyes since she knew full well that finding a decent guy in this town was a futile, frustrating task.

"*Bye*, Grandma," I'd said with an eye-roll as she cackled and clapped her hands.

I'm smiling now as I absentmindedly start opening white file-boxes that are neatly stacked in clearly separated rows, each row labeled with topics ranging from "Bills" to "Photographs" to "Clothes" to . . .

I blink as I stare at the last row of boxes, the memory of that final interchange with Grandma still lingering as I stare at the label and wonder if I'm hallucinating.

Given to the Groom

Yes, that last interchange, when Grandma almost seemed *pleased* that I was still single . . .

Like me being single fit perfectly into her plans . . .

Into her . . . unfinished business?

"Unfinished Business," I say out loud, raising my eyebrows and shaking my head as I read the words off the label. "Seriously, Grandma? You have a box labeled *Unfinished Business*?'"

I'm about to laugh, but I'm startled by a weird feeling of movement. It's like a breeze, but this is a closed attic, and I can't help but think back to that odd sense I got when I walked down the aisle . . . walked down the aisle alone but maybe not quite alone.

"Grandma?" I say out loud, more for my own benefit, to remind myself that honey, you're now seeing ghosts and hearing spirits. Could this get any more ridiculous. I cock my head and wait for a response, almost hoping there's a whisper from the afterlife or some shit. Then Grandma could just explain what the hell she was thinking, what she was planning before the heart attack, why she didn't *tell* me what she was planning?!

Was she gonna just spring it on me the day before the arranged marriage?

Was she gonna just ask me to meet her for coffee and then say, hey, I just *gave* you to this Greek mafia guy. Seeya! Send me a postcard from Mykonos!

Was she waiting till the last moment because she was afraid I'd say no?

I mean, of *course* I'd have said no, right?

Right?

"Right," I say, answering myself while trying to ignore that diamond ring on my finger, trying to ignore the unmistakably filthy feeling of Brakos's semen making its way out of me as I squat there on Grandma's floorboards and dig through a box that's labeled "Unfinished Business" like this is a fucking play being staged by those Greek gods that Brakos the Bold and Magnificent keeps going on about.

"The gods brought us together," Brakos had said. ""But now not even the gods can tear us apart."

His words send a wave of heat through me as I look through Grandma's box, and I almost sigh out loud as I'm aware once more of that steady, solid part of me that's somehow sure this is real, that's somehow certain Brakos and I are forever, that somehow understands what he meant when he said the facts don't matter when it feels like this . . .

"You were *given* to me, Bellanca," he'd said. "A gift for me. A gift. A gift."

"A gift," I say out loud as I look through what's in Grandma's box. At first it seems kinda what I expected: Copies of old Greek newspapers she must have gotten from some online library, printouts from random websites and even old magazines that she must have been collecting for years.

And notes. Lots of notes. All in her handwriting. Small and neat and kinda pointy, like her handwriting had the same edge Grandma did. Slowly I settle down and start to read her notes, read her mind, the mind of a scared young girl whose world had been destroyed.

A scared, *angry* young girl, I think as I read on, read faster, my eyes burning as I see what Grandma had been piecing together over years, decades, her entire life perhaps.

"Oh, Grandma," I say, clutching my heart as I feel that little girl's desolation, her anger, her rage.

Her need to know who killed her family.

And her need for revenge.

For justice.

Fucking payback.

"Oh, my God," I think, dropping the last page of notes and laying flat on my back as I gasp for air, struggle to come to terms with what Grandma had finally figured out after years of searching, decades of digging, back-and-forth between old libraries and convoluted red-tape and bureaucrats in Greece. "That's why you didn't tell me, Grandma. That's why you didn't tell me what you were planning! It's because you never intended the wedding to happen! You never planned to actually marry me off against my will! I wasn't a *gift* for Brakos! I was . . ."

And then slowly I sit up as I feel that spirit stir in the air even though I know it's just my imagination.

"No," I say, my eyes narrowing as if after reading Grandma's notes I've internalized her feelings, understood the kind of woman she was, understood the blood that ran in her veins, runs through *my* veins . . .

"I wasn't a *gift* for Brakos," I whisper as I look at the last page of Grandma's notes, where she puts it all together based on some old police reports she finally managed to get from some tiny office in Greece.

Reports that name her family's killers.

Killers who themselves were killed in an encounter with the Greek Police back in the 1940s.

Killers who left behind a daughter.

A daughter who lived a quiet life, married a quiet man, but remained childless until she herself was reasonably old, in fact past her child-bearing years.

She herself died in childbirth, but the child lived.

A miracle child.

A gift from the gods themselves.

A son.

Brakos.

My husband.

"Ohmygod," I mutter, glancing at my ring as that final piece of the puzzle fits together like a shard of glass that stabs me right through the heart. "I wasn't a gift for Brakos at all! I was . . . I was *bait*!"

I was bait.

The wedding *was* a setup. But not a setup for a marriage.

It was a setup for a hit.

I cover my mouth and start to laugh and sob at

the same time, shaking my head as I roll around in Grandma's attic like a freak. I don't know what the hell Grandma expected to do to Brakos once she got him to come to our town, but there's no way she could have pulled off a freakin' assassination no matter *how* badly she wanted to do it!

"Seriously, Grandma," I say through my hysterics. "I get the anger. I get the need for closure. Maybe I even get that twisted, old-world sense of justice where the son pays for the sins of the father. But really, Grandma. What could you have done against Brakos and an army of bodyguards?!"

"She could have done nothing," comes his voice, deep like the ocean, resonant like thunder. "But perhaps it was never her plan to do anything herself. Not when she had *you* to do it for her."

I sit up so fast I almost throw my back out. "Brakos?!" I yelp, pulling my knees up against my chest as he lumbers up the attic stairs, his body blocking out so much of the light it seems like the sun just set and night has fallen. "How long have you been here?!"

"Long enough to hear you talk to yourself," he says with a grunt, crouching so he doesn't bang his head on the low ceiling. He goes down on his knees and frowns as he flips through some of the Greek-language clippings and reports. Then his eyes go wide and his face almost drains of color. "*Apó ton Día*," he whispers. "She was right. According to this old report, it appears that the Belitrios Family was not in fact wiped out by the Sicilians. Even I did not manage to get this report when I looked into your family's history. Your grandmother knew how to squeeze things out of the past, did she not?"

I swallow hard as I see the grave expression on his face. I try to interpret the expression, but I can't quite put my finger on it. "Brakos, listen," I say, blinking and forcing a smile. "Let's take some time and sort through all this stuff, OK? Some handwritten report from ninety years ago isn't proof of anything. I mean, you would *know* if your grandparents murdered my great-grandparents, right? You'd never have fallen for Grandma's trickery, never have walked into a trap that would have been obvious. Or kinda obvious, at least. I think. I mean, I don't know what I think, but you know what I mean. OK, I'm babbling. I seriously shoulda eaten something. You didn't bring any food with you, did ya? Brakos? Why aren't you saying anything? Why are you looking at me like that? Brakos? Can you please say something? Can we talk? Brakos? Brakos?*Brakos*!"

9
BRAKOS

Brakos. Brakos. *Brakos*!

I hear her voice but I cannot respond. All I can do is look into her eyes as a feeling I cannot interpret invades me like a serpent slithering beneath my skin, coiling itself around my heart, my lungs, my throat from the inside until I feel like I'm choking.

"Blood is destiny, Bellanca," I mutter as pieces fit together so fast it makes me dizzy but also makes me smile. I shake my head as I gain control of myself, and now I feel a surge of power that reminds me that I *am* a god, that blood *is* in fact destiny! How else can this be explained!

"What the hell does that mean?" she says.

I take a breath and sit cross-legged in front of my wife, the woman I claimed as mine and will keep as mine, no matter what obstacles those mischief-makers on the mountain throw in our path. "Bellanca, listen. Listen carefully. No, I would *not* have known if my grandparents murdered your great-grandparents decades ago. I did not *know* who my grandparents were. Bellanca, I did not even know who my own parents were!"

She frowns and blinks. "I don't believe that. Weren't you going off about how you were descended from some old Greek mafia bloodline?"

I raise an eyebrow and grunt. "I said no such thing. Perhaps you are confusing me with your other mafia lovers."

She can't help but laugh. Then she sighs and takes a breath, raising an eyebrow and waiting for me to continue.

But I stay silent as I go through Bernice's notes. Notes from old Greek documents that must have taken years of painstaking effort to track down from paper records in government offices all over the old country. Then I exhale and speak. "Bellanca, I was raised in an orphanage in the Greek countryside. The orphanage had no clear records of my ancestry. Best I could tell my father had dropped me off and just walked away." I glance at the papers in Bernice Belitrios's box and then back into Bellanca's brown eyes. "And now I understand why. My mother died giving birth to me. My father either wanted nothing to do with raising me or perhaps even thought I was a curse, given I'd been born when my mother was past her child-bearing years. Greeks were a superstitious bunch back then. Who knows what went through his mind. I certainly didn't. Once I heard I was abandoned by my father, I made no further effort to understand my lineage. To hell with my parents, I'd promised myself as an angry young boy. I decided that Zeus himself was my father, and that was that. I was a god, and I was destined for greatness."

Bellanca moves closer to me as we sit huddled on the floor like schoolchildren, even though I'm about nine times her size—or so it seems in this cramped attic.

"So you . . . you worked your way up to the top of the Greek Mafia from nothing?" she says, and I swear I see a hint of admiration in her eyes before she quickly blinks it away.

I shake my head. "That's what I thought. But now I know I did not come from nothing. That is what I meant when I said blood is destiny, Bellanca. Do you see? It did not matter whether I knew the facts about my ancestry or who my grandparents were. My *blood* knew who I was, what I was born to be! My fate was determined by the blood that flowed through my veins. It was inevitable that I became who I am. My blood was my destiny." I pause and take a breath, shuddering as that dark feeling floods me again, that sickening but also exhilarating feeling I got when I understood what Bernice Belitrios was planning. "Just like *your* blood is *your* destiny, Bellanca. Your blood knows who you are even if your brain does not. And I think your grandmother understood this. She understood who you were, understood what she could awaken in you when the time was right, understood that you might be able to do what she obviously would never manage to pull off."

"Are you saying . . . you can't really believe that Grandma . . . that she . . . that I . . ." Bellanca stammers as the recognition dawns on her.

The recognition that perhaps her grandma was not just planning to use her as bait . . .

"I'm saying that not only were you to be bait for the trap that Bernice had set for me, but you were also the trap," I say softly, studying her face as I see the fire in her blood slowly rising along with the darkly invigorating self-awareness that I discovered in myself decades ago, when I first understood the kind of man I was.

And the kind of woman I'd need by my side.

"Not just the bait," she whispers through trembling lips. "I wasn't just the bait. I was also . . . also the weapon?"

I nod as I slowly back away from her, smiling as I see her come into her own like a goddess awakening. "Precisely. You were also the weapon, Bellanca. That was the final piece in Bernice's plan. She just happened to die before she put that piece in place. Maybe she wasn't sure how exactly to do it. Or maybe . . ."

"Maybe what?" Bellanca says, and I see her eyes narrow as she looks at me with a strength that gets my own blood hot, gets my muscles to coil, gets my fucking cock to stiffen.

"Maybe she believed that she wouldn't need to even do anything," I whisper. "Maybe she believed so deeply that blood is destiny, she simply trusted that she could just put you in a room with me and destiny would run its course."

"Destiny? What destiny? For me to . . . to *murder* you? To avenge something that happened generations ago, before either of us was even born? *That's* what you expect me to believe?! That's what *you* believe?!" She shakes her head and closes her eyes, swallowing hard like she's trying to fight herself, fight what's inside, fight what has to come out if she is to stand by my side, rule our empire with me, be the goddess to the god that I am. "Hell, you must be even dumber than I—"

I move so fast even I am surprised, and before I

know it I have her by the hair, my face close to hers. My own blood is boiling, but I am in control. I will not hurt her. This is about Bellanca, not Brakos.

"Brakos knows who he is," I growl against her cheek. "Brakos accepts who he is. Now Bellanca must do the same. Accept yourself, Bellanca. Accept that your destiny runs through your veins, is written in your blood. You cannot escape it, so you must embrace it." I kiss her cheek gently, my cock straining in a way that makes me want to take her brutally hard, fuck her to that place where she understands who she is. But I stay in control. I remind myself that this is about Bellanca and not Brakos. It is about her.

And it is about us.

"Blood is destiny," I whisper against her face. "You want proof? Then answer this question: Why did you get into that car, Bellanca? Why did you walk down that aisle, Bellanca? Why did you drink from that glass when I offered it? Why did you give yourself to me on our wedding bed? Why is my seed taking hold deep in your womb?" I pause as I feel her start to breathe hard. "And why do you feel what you are feeling right now? Why do you understand the legacy of violence that is in our blood, will be in our children's blood, will be passed on to their children . . . even if our own names are lost and forgotten with the passage of time."

She moans as I massage her neck, rub her breasts,

Given to the Groom

pinch her nipples so hard it makes my own fingers hurt. "What are you doing, Brakos? What am *I* doing? What am I *thinking*?!"

I kiss her hard on the lips, lifting her dress up over her arms and groaning when I realize she left our wedding suite without bothering to take her underwear. "You called me stupid twice today. But I am not stupid enough to fall for some fake documents describing some nonexistent criminal enterprise run by a ninety-seven year-old grandmother from her attic."

She pulls back for a moment. "Wait, you knew the documents were fake? Then why did you come? Why did you go through with the wedding?"

"I came for the one thing that was real, Bellanca," I whisper as I reach between her legs and slide my fingers into her wet cunt. "Almost every document Bernice sent me was a fake. But I did not care, because the one thing real was the proof of her bloodline, the proof of the blood that ran through her veins, runs through your veins."

"Um, that still doesn't explain a thing, Brakos. I still don't understand why you—"

"For the same reason you got into that car, walked down the aisle, took my seed into you, merged our bloodlines," I mutter. "We were drawn to each other by destiny: *Our* destiny, not that of our ancestors. There is a blood debt, yes. And your grandmother wanted it paid with blood, with death, yes. But the gods disagreed, and when Greek gods disagree, they intervene. Bellanca! The gods of old chose to give *our* destiny a chance to play out! We were put together by the gods to test each other, to complement each other, to love each other! Love each other forever, Bellanca. This is how the blood debt gets paid, Bellanca. Do you see? My ancestors took the lives of your ancestors. And now we will cancel the debt by creating *new* life."

"You realize that's circular logic, don't you?" she mutters as I push her down onto her back and start to rub her mound until she's dripping all over the floorboards. "You just said you had no idea who your grandparents were, so why did it matter if I was part of the Belitrios bloodline? Especially since you already knew there was no sprawling Greek-American mafia-network that you'd gain control of by marrying me."

"I did not know the facts of my ancestry or the blood-history that ties our families together, but I always understood that blood is destiny, Bellanca." I slide two more fingers into her slit as I raise my chin and look into her eyes. "And I knew that if Belitrios blood ran in your veins, it meant you were destined for something special, destined to be special. I was drawn to you, and it did not matter what else I got in the marriage arrangement. I did not *want* anything else, Bellanca. Just you. Only you."

"So you wanted my *blood*?" she mutters as she

spreads her thick thighs and I lick her with long vertical strokes, swallowing her tangy sweetness as my heat keeps rising. "Well, *that's* romantic. So you're a Greek vampire now? What happened to being a god? Vampire seems like a step down."

"You are talking too much, Bellanca," I growl against her pussy as I lap her wetness and then rise up and desperately get out of my clothes. "There is nothing more to be said. Nothing more to explain. Nothing more to understand." I toss away the last shred of clothing and then quickly flip her over, smacking her hard on the ass as she shrieks in shock. "But there is one thing to be done. It is a Greek wedding-night tradition. The claiming process is not complete until this is done."

I raise her ass and spank her good and tight. Then I spread her asscheeks and slowly lick her dark rear rim until she hunches over and gasps.

"You *cannot* be serious," she mutters. "A Greek wedding-night tradition? Brakos, there is no way you're . . . Brakos? Brakos? *Brakos*!"

10
__BELLANCA__

"**B**rakos? Brakos? *Brakos!*"

I hear myself screaming, but it sounds like a whisper as all my senses disappear just as Brakos slides his thick finger into my wet asshole and opens me up in the most filthy way imaginable. I moan and come all over my Grandma's attic floor as he slides his tongue deep into my rear canal, slicking me up all the way inside like the devil he is.

Given to the Groom

"Oh, fuck, Brakos," I groan as he pulls back and then firmly places his cock against my opening, sliding it slowly inside as I tighten, relax, and then submit with a shuddering sigh.

Submit to everything.

And then everything goes quiet as Brakos claims me from behind, and I close my eyes as I think back to that dark, twisted feeling that washed over me when Brakos went off about the whole blood-is-destiny stuff. I still don't know if I believe it. Still don't know if it's true, if it's real.

And then it occurs to me that I'll *never* know if it's "real" or not. Not in the way my brain wants to know. There are no "facts" that can prove that blood is destiny, that the two of us were drawn together by fate, put together by the gods.

I mean, there's that weird coincidence of a totally random wedding happening on the exact same day that Grandma chose for my arranged wedding.

Um, that *is* a weird coincidence, isn't it?

A coincidence that was just enough to have me downstairs waiting for a car to pick me up, just enough for me to let my guard down, just enough for me to . . . to . . .

To believe that the gods really are intervening?

That fate is real?

That blood is destiny?

Is that a fact or is it fantasy?

And does it matter?

No, it doesn't, I think as my husband shouts in Greek and comes deep inside me, his heavy balls slapping up against me as he empties them again until I'm overflowing with his seed. The facts don't matter anymore.

Because who needs facts when it feels like this.

Who needs facts when you know it's forever.

I close my eyes as Brakos collapses on me, squishing me onto the floor as Grandma's old papers float around us like confetti. I sigh as I wonder if I'll ever know what Grandma really expected would happen on our wedding day. Would she have pulled me aside and given me a vial of poison? Would she have slipped a gun into my panties? Or would she—like Brakos thinks—have simply trusted that I'd . . . what, just up and murder him because my "blood" would know there was a debt to be paid?

Brakos and I lie together in silence, and then I feel that weird sense of movement and my eyes flick wide open.

And immediately I turn bright red at the thought of what Grandma's spirit might have just witnessed!

But then I almost cry when I think that maybe she'd be just fine with it.

Maybe she'd understand that although her notes make it clear she carried hate and vengeance in her blood for decades, that she most certainly wanted

Brakos dead as payback for what his grandparents did to her family, that although I carried her blood in my veins, I also carry my own destiny in that blood.

A destiny that might be different from the one she envisioned.

"After all, Grandma," I whisper out loud as I look into my Greek god's green eyes. "This is America. We come here to escape the past, not to be bound by it, right? That's what freedom means, right? That's what America means. It's over, Grandma. The debt is repaid. The unfinished business is finished. Now and forever."

I listen for some sign, but it's quiet like a graveyard, and I decide that Grandma's spirit has either moved on or has fled the scene after seeing what just went down on the floorboards of her attic.

I close my eyes again, smiling to myself as I try to think of a future that's open-ended and free from the past. But something stirs in me, and I gasp when I look into Brakos's eyes, feel my blood move through my veins like it's a being with its own intelligence, its own fate, its own destiny.

Where will we be in thirty years, I wonder as Brakos caresses my cheek and mutters something about how I need to eat and then complains about the lack of Beluga caviar in my dead grandmother's attic.

But as we slowly dress and make our way down to the living room where I played as a child, my husband's hand in mine, his ring on my finger, his seed in my womb, I remind myself that it doesn't matter where we'll be thirty years in the future just like it doesn't matter where we were thirty or forty or a hundred years in the past.

The only time that matters is now.

The only place that matters is here.

Because in this place called here and now I've found my always, found my forever, chosen my destiny.

∞

EPILOGUE
THIRTY YEARS LATER
AN UNDISCLOSED LOCATION IN THE GREEK MEDITERRANEAN
BELLANCA

"I get to choose first this time!" squeals Brock, our five-year-old grandson who's the spitting image of Brakos. "She chose first last time!"

"I am the only one who chooses," comes Brakos's deep voice as he storms out of his study and snatches the bag of Turkish Delights from Benis, our four-year-old grand-daughter, who just stares wide-eyed at her mountain of a Grandpa.

Without even flinching Brakos walks to the open window and empties the contents of the bag into the wild blue Mediterranean sea that laps up against the old stone walls of this thirteenth-century monastery that we converted to . . .

To our headquarters.

Yes, headquarters.

Headquarters for a sprawling underground mafia operation that spans America, Europe, and is slowly making headway into Australia and Asia, if our talks with the Koreans go well.

And if our talks with the Koreans don't go well?

There's always the dark blue waters of the Mediterranean Sea to swallow the bodies, gulp down the evidence, clear the obstacles to expanding the empire that Brakos and I have built over thirty years . . .

Built together.

Built with blood.

I settle into my leather armchair and cross my legs as I watch our grandchildren howl and wail in protest at being deprived of *all* the candy.

I narrow my eyes and sigh as I watch my Greek god of a husband finally relent and sweep up his grandkids in his strong arms, whisking them towards the shining silver fridge built into the stone wall at the far end of the room.

"Beluga caviar," I hear him saying to them as they wrinkle their little noses up. "That is the only thing you are allowed to eat when in my palace. Say it. Beluga caviar. Beluga—"

The kids start howling again. But I don't intervene. I've raised four boys and nine girls already, and we run our household like we run everything. Hard. Tight. Fair but firm, like it's in our blood . . .

I sigh again as I close my eyes and touch my round belly Yes, thirteen kids in thirty years.

And there's a chance we aren't done yet.

Because although Brakos doesn't know it yet, I think I might be pregnant again.

Which is strange, since I coulda sworn I was past child-bearing years . . .

"Gods do not eat Turkish Delight," Brakos is saying to the kids as I focus in on whatever he's trying to teach them. "They eat Beluga Caviar."

And as I watch in amused silence, I see what I've seen with thirteen kids before these two:

Them looking up at Brakos and falling into line, the change happening with a strange suddenness, like something snapped into place, like they suddenly understood who they were, and that was that.

It happened with all the kids fast—maybe because

at that age your brain hasn't developed to the point where you second-guess your own body, your own instinct, your own blood.

It took me a while to get there, I remind myself as I reach for my tablet and flip through my encrypted messages, check on my shell companies, make sure the Swiss bank accounts are getting the deposits we're due . . .

Yes, it took me a while to get there, but I'm here now.

Here in that place where it feels like this.

Like always.

Like forever.

Like blood.

Like destiny.

Our destiny.

∞

OMG thanks for reading my craziness!
Love,
Anna.
mail@annabellewinters.com

∞